WOOD APE

C.G. MOSLEY

SEVERED PRESS
HOBART TASMANIA

WOOD APE

Copyright © 2018 C.G. Mosley

WWW.SEVEREDPRESS.COM

All rights reserved. No part of this book may be reproduced or transmitted in any form or by any electronic or mechanical means, including photocopying, recording or by any information and retrieval system, without the written permission of the publisher and author, except where permitted by law. This novel is a work of fiction. Names, characters, places and incidents are the product of the author's imagination, or are used fictitiously. Any resemblance to actual events, locales or persons, living or dead, is purely coincidental.

ISBN: 978-1-925840-16-2

All rights reserved.

PROLOGUE

1985, Baker County, Mississippi

Clifford Lowe, or Cliff as his friends knew him, had been searching for his fifth bullfrog of the evening when it happened. He'd spent the past hour knee-deep in the muck of Sanderson Swamp looking under every rock and inside every stump for the large amphibians. Frog legs were a favorite of his, and it was something he was quite accustomed to eating back when he lived in his native home of Baton Rouge, Louisiana.

It was a woman that had brought him to the quiet town of Dunn, Mississippi six months earlier. Her name was Jenny Fleming and when he'd first asked her about preparing a mess of frog legs, the woman wretched as if she were going to throw up. Cliff, appalled in his own right, decided at that very moment that he and Jenny would not work out. He was, however, suddenly stuck in the town of Dunn thanks to the new job he'd just accepted at the local textile plant.

With Jenny out of the picture, and nothing but time on his hands when he wasn't working, Cliff decided he'd waited long enough for a taste of the Cajun goodness well-cooked frog legs provided. Sanderson Swamp, named after the family that had once owned the land, was formed thanks to a family of beavers almost a century earlier. A small creek that could once be traced all the way back to a tributary of the mighty Mississippi River had provided the water, the beavers provided the dam. There had been efforts over the years to eradicate the pesky rodents, but in Cliff's best estimation, it seemed to him that the beavers had won.

With the sun beginning to set, and the clouds on the horizon beginning to turn a beautiful shade of violet, Cliff decided one more frog would be enough. He ventured to a section of the swamp he had not yet explored, hoping it would provide a quick find. Without realizing it, he was putting more distance between him and his truck. Cliff approached a hollowed-out tree trunk and reached for his flashlight. He was dismayed to find that it wasn't in its usual holster place...the holster attached to his belt. He glanced around him in all directions, deciding he must have lost it somewhere in the murky water. With the sky darkening, it would be next to impossible to see inside the tree without a light. For a brief moment, he considered returning to his truck for the spare light, but laziness got the better of him. Against his better judgment, he plunged a hand into the dark void of the trunk and felt around. It was full mostly of water and mud, but as he felt around something hard bumped against his hand. Cliff fought the urge to jerk his hand away, and instead wrapped his fingers around the object and pulled it out. It turned out to be nothing more than a snapping turtle, though it was quite large. The turtle snapped at him, and he suddenly realized it was an alligator snapper.

Could've lost a finger, he thought, and he cringed as he tossed the animal aside. In a few short minutes, his environment became much darker. Cliff pulled the trucker cap off his head and wiped the sweat away from his brow with his forearm. He sighed, his shoulders slumped. *I guess four will have to do tonight.*

Cliff reluctantly turned away and headed back in the direction that he'd come. He nearly tripped a couple of times over hidden tree stumps, rocks, and limbs all submerged underneath the water. Suddenly, it seemed eerily quiet. There wasn't the sound of a bird, insect, or other animal to speak of and something about the silence made him feel uneasy. Cliff tried to tell himself that his mind was playing tricks on him—that it had been that quiet all along and that his focus on finding dinner had been the reason he hadn't noticed it before. It wasn't just the silence...he seemed to *feel* a presence too. Just as he was about to reach dry land again, he heard it.

Cliff stopped in his tracks and whipped his head around in the direction of the sound. It was a ripping sound, but he couldn't place exactly what was being ripped. He turned his head back in the direction of his truck and something in the back of his mind was screaming at him to go to it quickly. For reasons that Cliff was never fully able to explain or understand, he instead turned and focused his attention again on the ripping sound roughly fifty yards away. There was light splashing he could hear too. Whatever was out there, it was in the water and it was large enough to create waves. Cliff looked down at his ankles as the water rippled past him. The ripping sound continued, and it beckoned him to investigate. Cliff trudged through the muck yet again and did so as quietly as he could. When he finally got close enough, the light was all but gone. Cliff crouched down behind a tree and glanced up at the sky. The stars were beginning to twinkle overhead. When he returned his attention to the thing making the sound, he squinted his eyes and a silhouette began to form in front of him.

The creature was kneeling, and it was clearly covered in hair. Cliff was unable to tell for sure due to the lack of light, but he thought it must've been brown in color. And it stunk. It smelled terrible…like that of decaying flesh. The hands it used to peel bark away from the tree were massive and looked similar to that of a primate. He could hear it breathing and the sound suggested whatever *it* was had large lungs to go right along with the rest of its large frame. Cliff's heart began to pound hard as his mind began to understand what he was looking at.

Bigfoot, he thought.

He must have watched the legendary creature peel bark off the tree for another two minutes before he finally figured out that it was retrieving insects and eating them. His knees began to ache, and he felt lightheaded, but he dared not move. A slight rumble in the sky drew Cliff's attention upward. There was a commercial airliner flying overhead and when he looked back toward the beast, it too had looked up. Not only had it looked up at the airplane, but it stood as well. The creature stood no less than 8 feet in height, its shoulders broad and hulking. The sight of the wood ape now standing on its feet scared Cliff so badly that he fell backward due to the dizziness that quickly overcame him. As soon as Cliff's bottom hit the water, the monster snapped its head around and glared at him.

With the aid of a sudden burst of adrenaline, Cliff began to propel himself backward while simultaneously rolling over onto his hands and knees. His frantic crawl forward quickly transitioned into him running away toward the truck. He did not look back, but he could hear the large beast stomping through the water after him.

It's chasing me, he realized with disbelief.

The wood ape growled at him and grunted something that sounded as if it were attempting to speak to him. Whatever it was trying to say, Cliff was uninterested. His concentration was on nothing else but getting into his truck and driving away as fast as possible. Much to his surprise, he somehow managed to outrun the beast to the truck and for the briefest moment, he thought that it had given up the chase. As he snatched the handle to open the door, he immediately realized he was mistaken.

A massive hand wrapped around his bicep and tightened like a vice. Cliff felt his feet leave the ground as he was jerked away from the truck and thrown through the air. When he crashed back onto the earth, he felt something *pop* in his left shoulder. The sensation made him yelp in pain, but he wasted no time returning to his feet and running again. With seemingly no other option, Cliff turned his attention to the nearby two-lane highway. If he could make it there, surely the elusive wood ape would give up on the chase.

It quickly became apparent that Cliff had managed to outrun the beast to his truck only because it allowed him to. With little effort, this time the wood ape caught up to him in mere seconds and wrapped its chubby fingers around his throat, jerking him backward again. Cliff felt his feet leave the ground and he kicked wildly with his heels, trying desperately to inflict any sort of damage to his attacker. Unfortunately, the wood ape's arms were long. Cliff's efforts were futile. Instead, the creature casually turned him around so that they were face to face. Cliff looked into the dark eyes that stared back at him and saw nothing there to suggest he would be granted any mercy. With his options running low, Cliff began to yell and plead for the wood ape to drop him and set him free. The beast responded by pulling him closer and sniffing at his face. Cliff winced and held his breath in an attempt to stifle the putrid smell. He felt the grip around his neck begin to tighten and came to the realization that the wood ape was about to crush his windpipe. He clawed his own fingers at the beast's, frantically trying to pry the massive hand away. The wood ape was undeterred and only tightened its grip further. Just as Cliff began to lose consciousness, he reached for his belt.

The next few moments felt like a dream, but he clearly felt the hilt of the knife in his hands. He felt his arm swing forward, though without his vision it was impossible for him to know exactly where the blade was going to land. It was only when the creature howled in pain and released its grip from his throat that his vision returned, and Cliff realized what had happened. The blade of the knife had somehow found its way directly into the right eye of the large creature. A shower of blood poured from the wound and the animal continued to wail pitifully.

Cliff gasped as his lungs begged for air. He fell onto his back and wriggled away from the carnage that was unfolding in front of him. For the time being, the wood ape didn't seem to be concerned with his presence, only with its own survival. It reached up, grabbed the hilt of the knife, and jerked it free from the gore that had once been a healthy eye socket. The beast momentarily glared at the human that had caused the injury but as the blood continued to pour from the wound, seeking vengeance at that particular moment was not a priority.

The wood ape retreated into the shadows of the forest, howling in pain as it moved away. Cliff, still unable to regain his footing, crawled away from the swamp. When he was finally able to walk again, he moved briskly back to his truck and sped away back to Dunn.

CHAPTER 1

35 years later...

Downtown Dunn, Mississippi looked as if it had somehow stopped moving at some point in the mid-fifties. There were no major chain stores of any kind to be found, and the same went for the restaurants. Every place of commerce that existed on the town square was locally owned, and many of the stores had been owned by the same family for decades. For those that happened to stumble upon its meager existence (no one really visited Dunn on purpose), at face value it appeared to be a charming little town...the sort of place one would picture on *Leave It To Beaver*, or *The Andy Griffith Show*. There were certainly shades of Mayberry no matter where you looked.

For Harry Schrader, the move to Dunn was largely his idea, though not for the reasons his wife thought. For all Lacey Schrader knew, the move to Dunn was a necessary evil of her husband's chosen profession. Harry was a high school principal, and the school where he'd worked in Atlanta, Georgia was forced to close its doors due to a state takeover. Harry was unfairly blamed for the school's consistently terrible test scores, but ultimately it had not cost him his job. There was an offer for him to take over as an assistant principal at a nearby junior high, but there were other matters that persuaded him to make a major move. Due to some pretty radical changes in his personal life, Harry decided it would be best to make a change to a smaller school district in a much smaller town. Due to time constraints, the move would be dictated by what was available, and what was available was an opening at a public high school in the Baker County school district of Mississippi.

Fortunately, Lacey's job as a paralegal was an easy move as well. It just so happened that one of the only two lawyers in the city of Dunn had just lost a paralegal. And "lost" unfortunately meant that 82-year-old Edna Fairchild had passed away of a sudden heart attack. As easy as the transition had been where finding work was concerned, it was equally easy for them to find what Lacey had referred to as *the home of her dreams*.

The house was a century-old antebellum two-story house, complete with four large ancient-Rome-inspired columns across the front of the antiquated structure. The price had been a steal in Harry's opinion, and when he asked the realtor to provide some insight for why the house was so cheap, she explained that there were many locals that believed the home was haunted. He and Lacey scoffed at the notion, as neither of them believed in that sort of nonsense. Their seven-year-old daughter, Alice, however, would most likely be terrified if she'd found out. It was explained that the previous owners had moved away suddenly, and the house was ultimately foreclosed on. Admittedly, when Harry considered the possible scenarios as to why the middle-aged couple would move away so suddenly, what the realtor said about the home being haunted vaulted to the forefront of his mind. When he'd brought the possibility up to Lacey, she immediately dismissed it. The expression on her face made it clear that she was smitten with the old house and he could see she was already decorating the place in her mind.

Aside from the beauty and history of the house, its location was probably the biggest selling point for Harry. Located in a secluded section of forest, and at the end of a red dirt road, the nearest neighbor was two miles down the road. The city of Dunn was a seven-minute drive. Close enough for convenience, yet plenty of distance to provide the privacy he desperately craved at this particular point in his life. Behind the home, probably a hundred yards away, an old red barn loomed large across the impressive landscape of meadow and pine trees. A boyish desire to venture inside the structure welled up inside of Harry, and he decided once they were all moved in, it would be the first thing that he explored on the property.

"Well, what do you think?" Harry asked, as Alice clambered up the front porch steps, her plush teddy bear clutched tightly to her chest.

Alice looked up at the enormous columns and followed them until they met the roof. "It's big," she said, sounding awestruck.

"Yeah," Harry said, glancing up with her. "It is definitely big. A lot of history in this old house." He placed a hand on the column nearest him and leaned against it. "It's a lot different from where we used to live. You're going to see a lot of nature's beauty here."

She looked at him, blinking. "Like what?" she asked curiously.

He smiled at her and knelt to her level. "Well, you'll see white-tail deer, turkeys, raccoons…maybe even a black bear."

Alice's green eyes suddenly widened, and a breeze blew a few of strands of blonde hair across her face. "Bears?" she asked with wonder.

Harry kissed his daughter's forehead. "Maybe," he said, though secretly he hoped not.

"What are you two up to?" Lacey asked, stepping out of the house behind them.

The movers were busy trudging in and out, pulling various pieces of furniture from their truck and placing them where she directed. They'd apparently taken a break.

"Mama, we're going to see bears!" Alice said excitedly, and she jumped off the porch, headed directly for the wood line.

"Stay where we can see you!" Harry called after her.

Lacey looked at Harry, bewildered, and then moved closer to put her arms around his waist. Harry didn't pull away from her, but he didn't seem to embrace her display of affection either. There was a coldness about him that Lacey was unable to figure out.

"Are you alright?" she asked, staying right where she was.

"I'm fine," he said, his eyes locked onto Alice.

"What's this about seeing bears?" she asked, looking up at him.

There was a hint of a smile, but it faded almost instantly. "Oh nothing," he said wistfully, still watching his daughter play. "Just her imagination running wild." Harry suddenly pulled away from her and glanced at his cell phone. "This isn't good," he muttered.

"What isn't good?" she asked, turning her attention to the phone.

"Cell service is terrible out here."

"Yeah, I noticed that," Lacey replied. "The phone company is coming out next week to install some updates to the landlines, but we'll have to manage until then."

Harry sighed, suddenly appearing very agitated. "There's no way to get them here any sooner?" he asked, pulling away. He made his way down the steps and held the phone up toward the sky, looking for improvement in the signal.

"No, I asked," she answered. Lacey placed her hands on her hips and stared at her husband a long moment before finally adding, "Are you expecting a call or something?"

Harry whipped his head around to look at her. "Maybe," he grumbled. "That a problem?"

Truthfully, it *was* a problem for her, but Lacey did not dare say it—at least not yet. She'd noticed her husband had become quite distant over the past three months. There were many instances of him walking around in their backyard speaking to someone on a cell phone. When she'd ask him who he was talking to, he would become quite defensive and almost angry. The uneasiness she felt about his private phone conversations were bad enough, but then there were the instances during the day where he would come up missing. She'd visited him at work on more than one occasion to find that he'd left early. No one in the school office seemed willing to tell her where he'd gone which only added to her suspicions.

He's cheating on me, she'd decided. It was a bitter pill to swallow, but she would not continue the charade for much longer. It was her hope that the change in their lifestyle would be of benefit to their marriage as well. But now, as her husband ventured further into the yard in desperate search for a signal, it seemed some things had not changed at all. Sooner or later, she'd be forced to confront him, but today was not the time.

Harry glanced over his shoulder to see if his wife was still watching. He could see that she was and despite what she thought about him, the way she looked at him made him feel quite shameful. He wanted to get it out in the open...to just tell her, but the timing was all wrong. There were a lot of decisions he needed to make, and they had enough going on with their lives at present without him adding something more to disrupt their lives.

Harry eyed an old pecan tree near the edge of the meadow. A pine thicket behind the tree seemed to be on the verge of overtaking the large tree. He made his way to the base of the tree and was pleasantly surprised to find that the signal on the phone picked up to three bars. He smiled as he took note of the time. He was beginning to worry that he was going to miss the call he was expecting, but fortunately, he had five minutes to spare.

Lacey kept her feet planted right where Harry had left her. Her eyes darted back and forth between her husband and her daughter. Each of them was on opposite sides of the meadow, but each of them required her attention at present. She wanted to tell Alice to move on the side of the meadow where her father was standing, beside the pecan tree. However, she was afraid if she did, Harry would potentially lose focus on his phone. She believed he was about to call someone but hoped fiercely that she was wrong. Harry paced back and forth for at least three minutes when suddenly, Lacey heard the phone begin to ring. Her shoulders slumped as she watched him answer. The conversation seemed serious. Lacey tried to picture what the woman he was talking to looked like and then, with a sense of painful dread building inside her gut, she reluctantly turned away to check on Alice.

CHAPTER 2

Lacey watched Alice play for almost half an hour before calling her into the house. Harry's phone call had only taken about ten minutes before he moped back. She couldn't help but notice how miserable he seemed, and she fought back the urge to cry. He literally moped up the steps that led to the front porch, his head hung low. She imagined the young, attractive woman that he'd been speaking to doing her best to coax him to leave her. As she considered this, her sadness turned into anger. She felt her face flush with heat and if it weren't for giving Alice a few minutes of play time, she probably would've barged in the house behind him and started World War 3.

When she finally *did* go inside, her cooler head prevailed and no sooner had the movers brought in the last piece of furniture did she announce that she was going to go into Dunn for a few groceries. Harry was sitting in the recliner, which had been placed at the end of the hallway. It was just one of many pieces of furniture resting in a temporary spot until Lacey could decide where everything would go. When she declared her intentions to drive into town, Harry looked at her, a clear sadness in his eyes. He mumbled a response though she could not fully understand it.

"Your daughter is upstairs playing," she said as he grabbed the car keys from the kitchen counter. "Try not to forget she's here," she added, annoyed.

Harry stared at her, somewhat curiously but said nothing. He just watched as she disappeared through the door. Once outside, she took note of the position of the sun and realized by the time she returned, it would probably be dark. She pulled the car onto the dirt road that led away from the house. As she drove through the dust that was still settling from the moving truck that had come before her, for the first time she realized how dirty her car would stay almost constantly. A dirty car was a pet peeve of hers and the thought of spending weekend after weekend washing the car made her head hurt.

When she rolled into the city limits of Dunn, she couldn't help but smile at the charming little town. The town square looked like something straight out of a novel or old television show. In the center of the square was a small park and she counted a grand total of four people and one dog currently enjoying the last bit of daylight. They waved at her and she waved back. As she continued, Lacey encountered other people walking along the sidewalks and every single one of them waved. The hospitality she experienced seemed to have a positive effect on her headache as the pain began to subside.

The grocery store wasn't hard to find and when she found it, she was a bit surprised at how many people were there. When she got out of the car to retrieve a shopping cart, she overheard two older ladies discussing an upcoming band of bad weather headed their direction.

"It'll be here late tomorrow," she heard one of the ladies say as the other shook her head, a look of worry etched on her face.

"Oh dear, I'll have to bring in my cats," the other lady replied.

Lacey smiled at them and moved into the store. She studied each face as she knew being in a small town she would encounter these people over and over. If they stayed there any length of time, she'd begin to learn their names and soon after she'd pick up on gossip. This was the nature of the beast in a small town, and Lacey thought she could get used to it...no matter how hard it was to keep the car clean.

The first thing she noticed when she got inside was an old man, resting against the counter that was usually reserved for a pharmacy that was currently closed. He had been looking at a newspaper stretched out across the countertop but paused to look at her when she moved past. His face was weathered, his eyes gray and watery. He wore a red baseball cap, and tufts of white hair poked out from underneath it in all directions. He turned his whole body to watch her as she strolled toward the bread aisle.

Lacey could feel his eyes watching her. It made her uncomfortable.

There were only four loaves left. She grabbed one and then did what was customary for the townsfolk of a small town to do when threatened with a storm: she moved on to get a gallon of milk. From there she moved down each aisle, picking up a wide variety of items. On the cereal aisle, she caught a glimpse of the old man watching her...seemingly following her. She snapped her head around to look at him. It was her hope that if she "caught" him following her around, he would become embarrassed and back off. To her surprise, he instead smiled at her and seemed anything but embarrassed.

"Can I help you?" she asked, unable to hide her annoyance.

Fortunately, a young stock boy was nearby, and he'd momentarily stopped, straightening the shelf containing pancake mix to see what the matter was. His presence made Lacey feel safe to confront the old man.

"Me?" the man replied, and he literally glanced to either side of him as if he were expecting to see someone else.

Lacey glanced at the stock boy. He shrugged in response. "Yes you," she said to the man, her tone softening a bit. "I'm sorry, I thought you were following me."

"I'm sorry," he answered, shifting his feet a bit. "I just haven't seen you before...and I know everyone in this town."

Lacey smiled and sighed. *Of course*, she thought. *It's a small town…I'm an outsider…*

"I'm new here," she told him. "Me and my family just moved in today."

The old man's face brightened substantially, and he moved closer. Lacey noticed he had a pronounced limp when he walked. "Well, welcome to Dunn," he said, beaming. "We're so glad to have you here."

"Well, thank you," Lacey replied, and she reached for a box of cereal.

"Where are you and your husband living?" he asked.

The stock boy drew near Lacey. "Ma'am, is he bothering you?"

She smiled at him and shook her head. "No, of course not," she answered. "But thank you." She turned to the old man and said, "We moved to the old antebellum home at the end of Isley Road."

The mention of where she lived made the old man stop dead in his tracks. The warmth in his face disappeared instantly and seemed to be replaced with something much cooler…something like fear. Lacey was confused, and she looked to the stock boy for some sort of clarification regarding the old man's reaction. She was dismayed to find that he too looked a bit uncomfortable.

"Umm…what's wrong?" she asked, her attention moving back and forth between the two men.

The stock boy took a deep breath and smiled. "Nothing...nothing at all," he said. "Welcome to Dunn."

"You're going to die," the old man said very flatly.

The stock boy's smile disappeared. His brow tightened. "Please do not frighten our customers."

"What? I'm going to die?" Lacey asked. "What are you talking about?"

"Your whole family will die...you need to get out of there...fast!"

"Sir, that's enough," the stock boy said. "If you can't stop frightening our customers, I'm going to have to ask you to leave." He then leaned close where only Lacey could hear him. "He's a bit nutty," he whispered. "He's known as the town crazy."

Lacey met the stock boy's eyes and she nodded. Suddenly, she felt a mixture of pity and sorrow for the old man. "I see," she said, returning her attention to the old man. "Well, thank you for the warning." She turned back to her cart and began to move away.

"Didn't someone tell you what happened to the former owners?" the old man said, and he took a step toward her again.

Lacey attempted to ignore him and moved in the direction of the checkout lines.

"They are dead!" the man said, his voice loud and powerful.

Lacey glanced around and could see other people in the store were now watching her. It was as if time had stopped and everyone else had their attention focused solely on her.

"If you don't get out of there, your family is going to die too!" the man added. He now made an attempt to chase after her, but his limp prevented him from moving very fast.

"Leave her be," the stock boy snapped. "Sir, you need to leave, right now!"

The old man paused and glanced at the stock boy and then to the other patrons in the store. "You all know it to be true," he said. "You all know she and her family is in danger...why don't you tell her?"

Lacey glanced around again at the other shoppers. They were all staring at her but said nothing. For a brief, awkward moment, Lacey stood in line behind a middle-aged man that was ahead of her checking out. He looked at her sadly as the cashier scanned one item after another. Lacey could *feel* the eyes of everyone watching her intensely. She could feel sweat beading up on her forehead. Her heart pounded in her chest. Her hands gripped the handle of the shopping cart so tightly that her knuckles turned white.

"They'll all die," the old man said again, and though she didn't look back at him, she could tell by the sound of his voice that he was moving closer to her. "Do you understand what I'm telling you, young lady?"

Suddenly, Lacey let go of the shopping cart, and snatched up her purse. She locked eyes with the cashier. "I'm terribly sorry," she said, moving toward the exit. "I feel sick, I need to leave."

The cashier nodded at her but said nothing. Lacey rushed through the exit and took a big gulp of the cool night air. She wasn't lying. She really *did* feel sick. She rushed to her car, her hands shaking. She heard the old man calling to her from across the parking lot. He seemed to be pleading with her to wait. Lacey ignored him and cranked the car.

CHAPTER 3

Harry wanted to chase after Lacey. He wanted to grab her by the arm, look her in the eyes and tell her the truth. The truth was killing him—and ironically it was the truth that was *literally* killing him. His biggest and most important concern was seeing the pain and hurt in her eyes—and then not being able to do anything about it. When she'd flashed in front of him and told him she was going into town, he could see a mixture of anger and hurt brewing behind her blue eyes. If he was going to tell her, he didn't want it to be in a moment where there was any hint of anger between them. No, he'd bide his time and wait for the right moment.

She hadn't slammed the door when she left, but she'd closed it with purpose. It was clear that she wanted Harry to know she was unhappy and she'd succeeded. For a few minutes, he sat there in near silence. The only sounds came from upstairs where Alice played. He contemplated going up to spend a few minutes with her, but truthfully, he didn't want to be around anyone. He shot a quick glance out the window closest to him and eyed the meadow. There was still an hour of daylight left so he decided to go outside and take a walk.

With the movers gone, the entire place had become unnervingly quiet. Harry moved across the tall green grass just as a gentle breeze blew across it. A terrible smell carried with the wind, so vile it almost made him wretch. He coughed and did his best to wave the horrible odor away from his face with his hand but to no avail. Harry turned in the direction from which the wind came and on the far side of the meadow he could see buzzards circling. Though he knew it was silly, he couldn't shake the feeling that someone was watching him.

The recent changes in his life had given Harry a newfound sense of fearlessness. He ignored the tiny voice in his head that screamed at him to return to the house, and instead casually strolled across the meadow toward the swirling birds. As he drew closer, the awful smell became worse. Harry pulled a handkerchief from his pocket and held it over his nose and mouth. His heart rate began to increase slightly as he began to seriously contemplate the possibility that he was about to discover a dead body on his new property.

Harry's thoughts again returned to Lacey as he walked. He considered their marriage, and all the happiness they had experienced over the past twelve years. In a matter of weeks, things had changed drastically. But had things gone too far? When Harry considered the things he could control, he didn't think so. No matter what his wife currently thought of him, he didn't want to lose her. He didn't want to lose Alice either.

When he was only twenty feet away, he began to hear the flies. The buzzing sound reminded him of the sound of high voltage at a power station. He slowed his pace...he wasn't sure why, but he still felt as if he was being watched. The dead thing—or what was left of it—was lying right where the meadow met the forest. Harry stopped within six feet of it, unable to get any closer due to the unbearable stench. He squinted his eyes, a desperate attempt to make sense of what he was seeing. Whatever he was looking at appeared to be nothing more than the innards of...something.

He didn't know a lot about the internal organs of humans, but he easily picked out many of the larger ones with ease. He could see lungs, a stomach, and even a heart. Suddenly, he felt lightheaded and momentarily thought he was going to pass out. His first day at his new home was seemingly turning from bad to worse. Again, he felt the nagging sensation that someone was watching. Harry whipped his head in all directions for any sign of life. Except for the buzzards and flies, he found none.

He began to feel the prickle of gooseflesh on his arms and neck. Harry turned away and headed back toward the house. Before he even realized it, he was running. After racing up the steps and through the front door, he headed straight for his cell phone. Alice came trouncing down the stairs, a doll in her hands.

"Daddy, I can't find Julie's clothes," she said, referring to the doll.

Harry glanced up after snatching his phone. "It's just packed up somewhere, hun," he replied. "We'll find it later." He began moving toward the door again. "Go back upstairs...I have to make a phone call."

Alice looked at him, bewildered, and then begrudgingly returned to her bedroom. Harry raced down steps and headed for the old pecan tree near the edge of the meadow. The sun would be gone in mere minutes and as he dialed the number, he suddenly wished he'd brought some sort of weapon out with him. The phone only rang twice before he got an answer.

"Baker County Sheriff's Department, what is your emergency?" an older woman said. She reminded Harry of his third grade English teacher Mrs. Turnbow.

"Yeah, I uh...I'm Harry Schrader, I just moved here today, and I found something strange on my property I think someone should come and take a look at."

"Where are you located, Mr. Schrader?" the woman asked flatly.

"I live at the end of Isley Road," he answered.

There was a pause.

"Are you there?" he asked.

"Yessir," the woman replied, and there was a change in her tone. Though it was slight, she seemed to be more concerned.

"I'm familiar with the property. I'm sending the sheriff right over."

"Thank you," he answered. He again surveyed his surroundings for anything unusual.

"Would you like to remain on the phone until he arrives?" the lady asked.

"No, that won't be necessary," Harry said. "I'll be watching for him...thank you for your help."

He hung up the phone and returned to the front porch. He decided he'd wait there, in the old rocking chair the previous owners had left behind. Darkness had now fallen and there was a chill in the air that seemed to be compounded by the strangeness of the last several minutes. In total, it probably only took the sheriff ten minutes to arrive, but it certainly felt longer.

When the patrol car came to a stop in his front yard, a man stepped out of the vehicle dressed in uniform...a tan shirt and dark brown pants. He wore a cowboy hat adorned with a gold star that matched the one on his chest. He appeared to be similar in age and build to Harry. There was a thick mustache under his nose.

"Good evening," the man said cheerfully.

"Good evening," Harry replied. He went down the steps to meet the man and extended his hand. "I'm Harry Schrader."

"Travis Horne," he replied, shaking his hand. Harry noticed Sheriff Horne look past him to the old antebellum house. "You just moved in?"

Harry nodded. "Just got here today," he answered.

"Well, welcome to Baker County," Sheriff Horne said. "We're glad to have you. Barb tells me you've got something here to show me."

"Yeah, I thought it best to have someone else look at this," he replied. "Come on...I'll show you."

As they moved across the meadow, Sheriff Horne pulled a flashlight from his belt and illuminated their path ahead. It wasn't long before he noticed what had drawn Harry to the site in the first place.

"Whew...something out here is dead," he said, waving his free hand in front of his face.

Harry said nothing and continued to lead the way. When they got close enough, he stopped and pointed.

"What's over there?" Sheriff Horne asked.

"I-I'm not sure," Harry stammered. "Just take a look."

Sheriff Horne moved forward with caution. When he finally got close enough, the flashlight illuminated the gore that existed in the tall weeds. "What in the world?" he said allowed, but he seemed unrattled.

"Is it...human?" Harry asked, sounding as if he wasn't sure he really wanted to know the answer.

The sheriff chuckled and turned back to look at him. "No, not at all," he replied. "It's from a deer."

Harry moved closer, so he could see. The flies were still buzzing, though they didn't seem as active as before. "You're sure?" he asked, sounding unconvinced.

"Pretty sure," Sheriff Horne replied confidently.

"Well, what's it doing here?" Harry asked, dumbfounded. "Did some animal do that?"

"No," the sheriff said. "But I think I know what happened." He paused and looked around as if he were suddenly spooked.

"What's wrong?" Harry asked, noticing the sheriff's sudden concern.

"We better go inside," Sheriff Horne said. "I'll explain everything."

CHAPTER 4

Lacey contemplated driving to a neighboring town to get the items she'd intended to buy at the grocery store in Dunn. It wasn't that it couldn't wait until morning, it certainly could. She was more concerned about returning home empty-handed. If that happened, she'd almost certainly be asked why by Harry which in turn would mean she'd have to engage him in conversation. She wasn't feeling very chatty at the moment, least of all with Harry. The nearest grocery store (that she knew of) was about thirty minutes away from Dunn. Lacey was already overcome with exhaustion and just wanted to go home, lie down, and go to sleep. After weighing her options, she ultimately decided she'd return home. If Harry spoke to her, she'd keep it short and to the point.

She took her time driving back, even poking along Isley Road to give Harry every opportunity to become preoccupied with something, so she could avoid him. As the antebellum home grew larger in her windshield, its brilliant white contrasting against the dark sky, something else caught her eye that immediately troubled her. Parked in the driveway next to Harry's truck, was a Baker County Sherriff's Department patrol car. Suddenly alarmed, Lacey increased her pace significantly before finally coming to a sliding stop in the gravel driveway. She raced up the steps, doing her best to remain calm, and then burst into the house.

"Harry?" she called, closing the door behind her. "Harry, is everything alright?"

She heard footsteps coming from the kitchen and suddenly he appeared. He was very calm which immediately calmed her.

"Everything's fine," he said. "Calm down."

"I'm calm," she replied.

There were more footsteps and a tall man with a cowboy hat and mustache appeared from behind her husband. "Good evening, ma'am," he said, removing his hat.

Lacey looked at him and for a brief silly moment, she wanted to laugh. Something about the way he took his hat off and referred to her as *ma'am* humored her. The man stood there for an awkward moment, his hat in his hands. He stared at her and then back to Harry.

"Oh, I'm sorry," Harry said, suddenly remembering his manners. "Lacey, this is Sheriff Travis Horne...Sheriff, this is my wife, Lacey."

"Nice to meet you," she replied curtly. "Did you come by to welcome us to the neighborhood?"

Sheriff Horne smiled, and shook his head. He glanced at Harry.

"I called him," Harry said. "I found something odd and I just wanted someone to come check it out."

"Oh?" she said, a mixture of confusion and concern on her face. "What did you find?"

"Nothing to be worried about," he replied. "Just a dead deer at the edge of the woods."

Lacey raised an eyebrow. "You called the sheriff's department to look at a dead deer?"

Sheriff Horne stepped forward. "Well, actually, it was just the innards of a dead deer."

She made a sour face. "I'm sorry, did you say the *innards*?"

The sheriff's eyes widened, and he grinned. "Yes, ma'am...it's guts...it's uh...its internal organs..."

"Sheriff, I know what innards are," she snapped, cutting him off. She hated it when a man spoke to her like she was a child. "What animal would leave a deer's..." she paused, considering the right word. "Guts...would what leave a deer's guts out in the open like that?"

"No animal I know of," Sheriff Horne replied.

Lacey stared at him, and when he said nothing, she looked to her husband.

"Okay," she mumbled. "Harry, what could have done that?"

"Well, the sheriff here seems to think it was some of our neighbors," he answered.

"The Conner brothers," the sheriff explained. "They live a couple of miles away...through the woods," he added, jerking a thumb toward the backside of the meadow.

"So why would they be dumping deer guts on our property?" Lacey asked.

"My guess is that those boys have been doing some hunting in these woods," he said.

"So, they're trespassing?"

"Yes, ma'am, they certainly were trespassing when they dumped the deer remains, but the worst of it is that it's not even hunting season anymore. They're hunting illegally and the first call I'm going to make in the morning will be to the Mississippi Department of Fish and Game."

Lacey sighed and crossed her arms. "So, let me get this straight. We've got a couple of punks running around in the woods behind our home with a gun...correct?"

Sheriff Horne looked at her curiously. "Yes, ma'am, I suppose that's probable."

"And the best you're going to do is call the local game warden tomorrow?" she asked, clearly annoyed. "Sheriff, I've got a young daughter that spent all afternoon playing in that meadow."

Harry swallowed and move toward his wife. He gently placed a hand on her shoulder. "Lacey, you're tired and I think you're overreacting just a bit."

She snatched her shoulder away. "Overreacting? No, I don't think so. Sheriff, I'd feel a lot better if you at least go over there and have a chat with the Conway brothers and give them a good talking to."

"*Conner* brothers," Sheriff Horne corrected her.

Lacey shot him an icy stare. The sheriff held up his hands in surrender.

"But your point is well taken," he said sheepishly. "I'll go by and talk to them first thing tomorrow…that's a promise."

"Thank you," she replied, her mood softening. "Generally, are these brothers troublemakers?"

Harry chuckled. "Honey, they've only been hunting in the woods. I don't think that—"

"Actually," the sheriff cut in. "I'm not gonna lie to you folks, they are what I'd call troublemakers, yes."

Lacey gave Harry an *I told you so* glare and then asked, "Sheriff, are these young men dangerous?"

Sheriff Horne smiled and waved her off. "No, ma'am, absolutely not. They cut up and get into all kinds of shenanigans, but they wouldn't intentionally hurt anyone. That much I'm certain about."

Lacey breathed a sigh of relief and nodded her head. "Okay, good."

Sheriff Horne looked to Harry and held out a hand as he returned his hat to his head. "Mr. Schrader, it was a pleasure to meet you, but I think I'm going to head on out now. You've got my number so don't hesitate to call when you need me."

"Thanks," Harry said. "I appreciate you coming out so quickly."

"No problem," the sheriff said and then he turned to Lacey. "Ma'am, I'm gonna talk to those boys...that's a promise."

"Thank you, Sheriff," she said. Lacey smiled at him...a gesture meant to let him know she was truly appreciative and she didn't intend to be difficult.

Just as he reached for the doorknob, Lacey threw a question out that made him stop dead in his tracks. "Sheriff, what happened to the previous owners of this house?"

Harry looked at his wife, confused, and then to Sheriff Horne who was slowly turning back to face them. "You don't already know?" he asked.

"Yeah," Harry answered. "The realtor told us that they just moved away suddenly."

The sheriff smiled. "Well, there you go," he said.

Lacey stepped toward him. "Then why did a man just tell me that they died?" she asked, raising an eyebrow.

Sheriff Horne took a deep breath and let go of the knob. He scratched at the back of his head and shifted his feet. Suddenly, he seemed nervous. "Who told you that?" he asked.

"It doesn't matter," she said. "Is it true?"

"No," he said a little too quickly. "No one knows for sure what happened to them…they just vanished."

Harry asked, "Does it have something to do with this house being haunted?"

The sheriff chuckled and looked around at his surroundings. "I don't think so…well, maybe," he added. It sounded more like a question than a declarative statement. "Why, have you seen something?"

"No," snapped Lacey. "We haven't seen anything because this house isn't haunted. So why would they just take off and leave? Are you certain they're not dead?"

"Of course not," Sheriff Horne replied. He was beginning to sound slightly angry. "No one knows for certain what happened to them. They were here one day and then the next they were gone. They left everything behind but there was no sign of foul play…nothing at all."

"And that doesn't concern you?" she asked.

"Of course it concerns me!" he shouted at her.

Lacey took a step back, startled by his drastic change in character. Harry stepped in front of his wife. "Sheriff, calm down," he said, holding up a hand.

Sheriff Horne was breathing deeply, and he seemed to suddenly realize what he'd done. An expression of embarrassment washed over him. "I'm sorry," he said gently. "I didn't mean to lose my cool." He paused and removed his hat, holding it in both hands. "As I said, no one knows for sure what happened to them. They were a nice older couple and their disappearance was a shock to the whole town."

"Alright, sheriff," Harry replied. "We believe you. Again, I thank you for coming out so quickly tonight. I'll call you again if I run into another problem."

Sheriff Horne nodded slowly, and he glanced at Lacey. Her arms were crossed, her mouth a straight line. She clearly wasn't as forgiving as her husband. He returned the hat to his head, and then turned to open the door. When he stepped out onto the porch, he glanced over his shoulder at them.

"I meant what I said, Mr. Schrader. If you need anything, you call me, and I'll come running."

"Thank you, Sheriff," Harry answered.

Without another word, Sheriff Travis Horne returned to his patrol car and disappeared into the night.

CHAPTER 5

"Did we just make a terrible mistake?" Lacey asked.

Sheriff Horne was now gone, but the tension he'd left still hung thick in the air. Harry had anticipated a fight when his wife returned, but after the strange interaction with the sheriff had occurred, Lacey's attention seemed to have shifted.

"What?" he asked, unsure of what she was referring to.

"This," she replied, and she glanced around the living room. "This house...I'm starting to seriously regret moving here."

Harry chuckled. "It's only the first day," he said. "You fell in love with this house."

"Yeah, I did," she said, and she walked past him toward the stairs. "I'm starting to think that maybe it's too good to be true. This doesn't feel right."

Harry followed her. "I admit we're not off to the best start, but we need to give it more time than one day."

Lacey stepped toward him and jabbed a finger into his chest. "You've got to be kidding me," she snapped. "You've barely spoken to me since we've arrived here. You have acted like you're miserable here and you'd rather be anywhere else *but* here."

Harry stared at her, unable to speak for a moment as he realized what he'd hoped to avoid was suddenly happening. "I- I'm sorry," he stammered. "I've just got a lot on my mind."

Lacey's expression softened slightly, and she touched his forearm. "That's been obvious so why don't you tell me what's going on? Stop hiding things from me. Whatever it is, you can tell me, we'll work through it."

There was a pain in her eyes, a pain that made Harry's heart ache. He wanted to tell her badly, just to get it out in the open, so they could get on with their lives. It wasn't fair to keep hiding it from her.

"It's…it's nothing," he said, looking away.

Lacey pulled back from him, the softness in her face slowly hardened into anger. "If it's nothing, then why can't you tell me?"

Harry said nothing, he just shook his head and stared at the floor.

"You coward," she snapped, turning away from him. She stomped up the stairs.

"Please try and be quiet," he called after her. "Alice is asleep."

Lacey said nothing, but disappeared into their bedroom, closing the door behind her. Harry stood there in the living room for a few minutes, his hands in his pockets. He contemplated what the sheriff had said and what Lacey had said about someone telling her that the previous owners had died. Sheriff Horne certainly seemed as though he was hiding something. He'd become angry when pressed and the reaction did little to ease Harry's mind about the remains he'd found at the edge of the woods.

He heard the sound of water above him and realized Lacey was taking a shower. It was his hope that by the time she was finished, the anger she was feeling toward him would've subsided enough that he could talk to her. None of what he was going through was his or her fault, but he felt guilt nonetheless. He still loved her, there was no denying that. It would be up to him to explain it to her and make it as painless as possible.

Harry made his way up the stairs and paused a moment to peek into Alice's room. She was in an obvious deep sleep, her flowered nightgown rising and falling with every soft breath. He felt a knot tighten in his stomach as he considered how what he was going through would affect her. It was hard for *him* to imagine a world where the three of them would not be together every day. So, for Alice, a change like that would be devastating. He stood in the doorway and watched his daughter until he heard Lacey turn off the shower. He waited a few more minutes to give her time to get dressed before finally gaining enough courage to go and make another attempt to talk to her.

When he entered the bedroom, she was already in bed flipping through a magazine. She paid him no mind when he entered the room. Harry made his way around the bed and sat down beside her. There was a long awkward silence.

"I'm sorry," he said finally.

"Sorry for what?" she asked, flipping another page.

"I'm sorry for putting you through this," he muttered.

He heard her take a deep breath and put the magazine aside. "You don't have to be sorry," she replied. "Just talk to me, Harry."

Harry glanced over at her. "I don't want to hurt you," he said.

Lacey stared at him and he could see her eyes begin to well up with tears. "I already know, Harry," she said, her voice cracking.

He stared at her bewildered. "You do?"

She nodded and began to cry. "You're having an affair," she said. "It's been going on for a couple of months and I've done my best to ignore it in hopes that you'd come to your senses. But it just hasn't happened."

Harry was taken aback. "Lacey, I—"

"And then today...a day that was supposed to be full of happiness and excitement...you spent a great deal of time looking at your phone. You were waiting on her to call you. It's pretty obvious you'd rather be anywhere but here."

"Lacey, please calm down," he said. "You're getting louder and Alice—"

"I don't care," she snapped, sobbing. "And speaking of Alice...how could you do such a thing to her?"

"Let me talk," he said, but she interrupted him again.

"No, you've had your chance to talk about this and you've squandered it over and over. Now you can listen to me," she said. "If you want a divorce, then let's get on with it. I'm not going to continue to turn a blind eye to what you're doing."

Harry stood up suddenly and though he wanted to discuss the matter further, he could feel *it* coming.

"What's wrong?" Lacey asked, still sounding angry.

Harry ignored her and briskly walked into the bathroom. No sooner after he closed the door, he began to cough. It was soft at first but soon evolved into a violent display that brought him to his knees. He reached onto the countertop for a hand towel to cover his mouth, a desperate attempt to muffle the sound.

"Are you alright?" Lacey asked from the other side of the door.

Harry wanted to respond but was unable to. He closed his eyes and concentrated hard on regaining control of his body. He breathed in deeply through his nose and slowly the coughing fit began to subside. When he finally felt it was safe enough, he tossed the towel onto the floor, and stood back up. Harry then turned on the cold water and leaned over the sink, cupping water in his hands and drinking.

"Harry, answer me," Lacey pleaded. "Are you alright?"

"I'm fine," he said once he'd stopped drinking. He reached over and opened the door.

"I thought you were choking," she said, looking at him wide-eyed.

"Don't know what came over me," he replied, with a weak smile.

"Are you sure you're alright?" she asked again.

Harry nodded. "Yes, sorry I scared you."

He followed her eyes as they watched him with obvious skepticism. They slowly moved away from him and toward the floor. It was then that her eyes widened yet again, and her mouth dropped.

"What's wrong?" he asked, confused.

Her eyes darted back up to his. "Harry, what is wrong with you?" Her face had turned ashen.

"I told you," he said, still confused. "I don't know what came over me."

Lacey said nothing, but instead pointed toward the floor behind him. Harry craned his head around and then he noticed his mistake. The towel he'd used to muffle his cough was covered in spatters of blood. When he looked back at her, she was crying again.

"Oh my God," she whispered.

Harry sighed and shook his head in disgust. "This wasn't how I wanted you to find out," he grumbled.

Lacey opened her mouth to speak, but a scream interrupted her. It was Alice. Harry ran past his wife and into the hallway. When he reached Alice's room, he burst into the room and turned on the lights. Alice was sitting straight up in the bed, a teddy bear clutched tightly against her chest. She was shaking and looked as if she'd seen a ghost.

"What's wrong?" Harry asked. Lacey moved past him and sat onto the bed beside their daughter. She put her arms around her and looked up at her husband.

"She's shaking like a leaf," she said.

"Something is outside my window," Alice stammered.

Harry's brow tightened, and he moved toward the window, jerking the curtains aside. Alice jumped when he did so as if she were expecting something to be waiting on the other side. There was nothing but the darkness of the night.

"I don't see anything," he said, leaning forward and peering in all directions.

"S-something was tapping on the window," Alice said.

"Something or *someone*?" Lacey asked, and she glared at Harry.

"We're on the second story," he answered, realizing she was referring to the Conner brothers. "They'd need a ladder to get up here and that's an awful lot of trouble to go through to just to pull a prank."

"They could've been throwing rocks or something," she countered. "They know we're new here and they're screwing with us," she added, sounding certain.

Harry stared at his frightened daughter and worried wife. It was certainly possible that the Conner brothers were indeed lurking around their house laughing in delight at the mischief they were causing. If they were still out there, he needed to put a stop to it before this got any worse.

"I'm going outside," he said suddenly, and he headed for the door.

"No, Daddy," Alice said. "Don't go out there, *it* might get you."

"Not *it*, honey, but *who*," he replied. "And if it's who I think it is, they're harmless, just stupid."

Lacey stood up and moved close enough so only he could hear. "Are you sure this is a good idea?" she whispered. "Don't you think we should just call Sheriff Horne back?"

"No," he answered, and he trudged down the stairs. "I'm putting a stop to this now."

"And just what do you plan to do?" Lacey asked.

"Hopefully scare them worse than they're scaring us," he answered.

CHAPTER 6

Harry grabbed two things before he went outside: a flashlight and a baseball bat. It was cool outside, so much so that he could see his breath. He paused on the front porch and listened for a sound. Harry expected to hear young men laughing or the sound of someone retreating into the woods. He decided he wouldn't chase after them if that were the case, and instead he'd probably take Lacey's advice and call the sheriff back. However, if they were still lurking around him home, he'd confront them and hopefully put a stop to any future problems. There was a fog rolling over the meadow and though there was supposed to be a full moon out, it was hidden away behind dark clouds.

Once he'd listened for a couple of minutes and heard nothing, he decided to move around the house to investigate. Harry turned the flashlight off and moved toward the right side of the house, the bat clutched tightly in both his hands. When he rounded the corner, he squinted his eyes hard in search of a silhouette or any sort of movement. He found nothing, but the shadows against that particular side of the house were thick and could easily provide cover for anyone—or anything—that could potentially be hiding there. Harry made a full lap around the house and after finding nothing, he decided he'd go and investigate the side of the house where Alice's window was.

As he walked, Harry continued to move the flashlight back and forth in front of him in a wide swath. The flashlight dangled beside him, clutched tightly in his right hand. He was not a violent man and strongly hoped he would not have to use it. His ears strained as hard as his eyes, desperately trying to sense something out of the ordinary. When he reached Alice's window, he looked up toward the second story, his light following the direction of his gaze. At first, he didn't notice it, but as the light moved back downward toward the ground, it caught his eye.

"What the hell?" he said aloud, moving toward it.

On the wall, directly in front of him, there was the unmistakable shape of a handprint. It was muddy and showed up easily against the white paint. Harry moved toward it and placed his own hand on the wall beside it. The print was enormous, at least twice the size of his own hand. The realization of what he was looking at suddenly startled him and he immediately jerked his hand away and whipped around to see if something was approaching him from behind. Once he was satisfied he was still alone, Harry moved the light up the wall and noticed another handprint higher up, only a few feet below Alice's window.

Whoever had been tapping on her window had gone to a lot of effort to do it.

But why? he wondered.

Harry stood there staring at the strange prints for a few minutes before finally moving his investigation to the ground around him. It was his hope he'd find a footprint, but there was nothing but grass all around. Suddenly, he heard a sound above him and he glanced up to find that Lacey had opened Alice's window and was peering down at him.

"Everything alright?" she asked.

Harry could see the worry in her face and he watched her eyes drift past him, searching for some sort of nearby danger. "Everything is okay," he said. "Close the window and go back inside."

"You need to come back inside," she called down to him, but her eyes were still scanning over the meadow behind him.

"I'll be up in a minute," he replied. "See if you can get Alice back to bed. Everything is alright out here."

He watched her sigh, but she said nothing. Seconds later, the window was closed, and he found himself alone yet again. Harry contemplated whether he should tell Lacey about the strange prints on the side of the house. She was already on edge and he wondered if it would do more harm than good to tell her. Clearly, she didn't trust him and keeping this from her would do nothing to help that fact. Most likely he'd call Sheriff Horne in the morning and have him look at the prints and at that point he'd have no choice but to tell her. It could wait until in the morning he finally decided, and he trudged back toward the front porch. He'd only taken two steps when he heard it…a loud crash near the back corner of the meadow.

Harry stopped dead in his tracks and whirled around with the flashlight. It came from the old barn. He stood there, his heart pounding as he contemplated what to do next. Every fiber in his being was screaming at him to retreat back into the house, get his phone, and call the sheriff back out to investigate. Harry glanced down at the bat that dangled at his side.

No, he thought, a surge of courage welling up within him. *I can take care of this myself.*

Before taking a moment to consider his options further, Harry found himself walking at a steady pace in the direction of the barn. As he drew nearer, he flicked the flashlight off and shoved it into the back pocket of his pants. With both hands now free, he wrapped both around the bat and wrenched it tightly in his grip. His heart continued to pound, but strangely, there was no fear. With the largest challenge of his life now looming, this was going to be a piece of cake. He had no intentions of actually beating the Conner brothers with the bat, but he certainly intended on making them *think* he was.

As he got within a few feet of the barn door, Harry slowed his pace dramatically. There was another rustle of movement from behind the door, but Harry continued to move forward. He reached for the handle, and the door suddenly swung open, striking him on the side of the head. Harry fell backward but kept his eyes on who—or what—was coming after him. He caught a glimpse—a silhouette—of a person bearing down on him. Without hesitation, Harry swung the bat at the man's leg and he instantly collapsed with a howl of pain.

Harry drew back for another scream, but the man yelped at him.

"Stop—stop!" he cried. "Are you nuts?"

Harry immediately refrained from swinging the bat again as he suddenly recognized the voice that was pleading with him.

"Dwight?" he asked, dropping the bat beside his leg. "Is that you?"

"Of course, it's me," Dwight grumbled. "Is this any way to greet your brother-in-law?"

Harry offered his hand and pulled Dwight from the ground. "What the hell are you doing hiding out here in the barn?" he asked, sounding a bit angry and relieved at the same time.

"I got my reasons," Dwight said, and Harry could see him rubbing at his forearm.

"Are you alright?"

"Yeah, I think so," he answered. "I don't think it's broken."

"I'm sure you'll have a nice bruise," Harry said. "I still want to know why you were hiding out in my barn."

He could hear Dwight sigh, the kind of sigh that suggested he was annoyed by the question. "I was hiding out here because I didn't want to disturb you guys," he said. "It was dark, and I shut my bike off at the end of the road, so you guys wouldn't hear. I knew Alice was probably in bed and I just didn't want to make a bunch of racket."

"And you couldn't call us?" Harry asked.

"I tried," Dwight answered. "It kept going to voicemail. Cell service sucks here."

"Yeah, it does," Harry agreed. "What are you doing here?"

Dwight sighed again, this time he sounding a bit embarrassed. "Well, you know," he said, and he rubbed his boot in the dirt. "I'm a drifter...I really ain't got a home and I was wondering if I could crash here a couple of days."

Harry crossed his arms and shook his head. It was true, Dwight was a drifter. He'd been all over the country on his motorcycle performing odd jobs in various towns. He'd been in trouble with the law multiple times as well. Harry could never decide if he liked Dwight or not, but Lacey always seemed sympathetic and protective of him. And despite what he thought of him, Dwight had always been kind and gentle with Alice.

"How did you find out where we were?" he asked. "We just moved here today."

The silver moon had finally peeked out from behind the dark clouds, and the illumination showed Dwight's teeth when he smiled. "Mom told me," he said.

"That figures," Harry said.

"I'm sorry, Harry, I didn't mean to cause any trouble. If you want me to move on, I'll be—"

"Don't be ridiculous," Harry interrupted. "Get your stuff and come inside. We can discuss this some more in the morning."

Dwight stared at him. "I don't know, man," he said.

"Well, I do," Harry said. "Get inside; you can sleep on the couch."

Dwight looked over his shoulder back into the barn. Something seemed to be troubling him.

"Your bike will be fine," Harry said, rolling his eyes. "Come on, let's go."

Dwight snapped his attention back to Harry, the smile on his face returning. "Yeah...okay," he said. "Let's go inside."

CHAPTER 7

By the time Harry and Dwight returned to the house, Alice was asleep, but Lacey was waiting and eager to learn what her husband had seen. She was incredibly surprised to find Dwight trailing after Harry, and after a brief explanation, they all decided to call it a night and discuss the matter further in the morning. The rest of the night lacked further interruption and the following morning, Harry was awoken by the smell of eggs and bacon sizzling in the kitchen.

He trudged down the stairs, yawning and stretching as he went, and ultimately found Lacey and her brother catching up in the kitchen.

"Good morning," Dwight said, and he held up a cup of coffee to greet him.

"Morning," Harry replied. He retrieved a cup and poured himself some orange juice. Meanwhile, Lacey was at work over the stove.

"Sleep well?" Dwight asked as Harry took a seat across the table from him.

"I did," he answered. He took a long pull of orange juice and wiped his mouth with the back of his hand. "How about you?"

Dwight smiled. "It was a heck of a lot better than that dirty barn was gonna be," he said. "Although my forearm is a bit swollen," he added, showing his arm.

Harry nodded, his mouth a straight line. "Yeah, I said I was sorry about that," he said.

"Well, it doesn't hurt you to say it again," Lacey quipped. She kept her back turned and continued about her work over the stove.

"No need for that," Dwight said. "I know I gave Harry a bit of a scare, and I would've done the same thing in the same situation."

There was a moment of silence and the two men stared at each other. Lacey abruptly turned and placed a plate of bacon and eggs in front of each man. "Eat up," she said.

Her husband and brother smiled at her and wasted no time digging into the meal. Harry bit off a piece of crispy bacon and as he chewed, he asked, "Dwight, were you peeking in any windows last night when you got here?"

Dwight was just about to place a fork full of egg into his mouth. The question caught him off guard and he returned the fork to the plate. "Umm…no, I don't think so," he said. He glanced at Lacey, hoping for some sort of explanation.

"Are you sure?" Harry pressed.

Dwight shrugged and smiled sheepishly. "No, I didn't peek in any windows. I'm pretty sure I'd remember it if I did," he said, again looking at his sister. "Why are you accusing me of that?"

"Alice heard a sound outside her window last night and Harry went out to check it out...that's why he was outside," Lacey explained.

"Oh, I see," Dwight said, and he turned his gaze toward Harry. "I promise you, I didn't do anything around the house. I did exactly what I told you...I shut the bike off at the end of the road and as soon as I saw the barn, I made a beeline for it. I didn't want to wake you guys up."

Lacey sighed and took a sip of coffee from the yellow mug she'd been holding. Her eyes were red, and she looked exhausted. "I'm sure it was nothing," she said. "Probably the wind or something."

"It wasn't the wind," Harry said. He was staring at his plate.

Lacey took another sip and asked, "Well, then what was it?"

"There were a couple of muddy handprints on the wall," Harry explained. "Something was trying to climb up to Alice's window."

Lacey's eyes widened, and she put the coffee mug down on the table. "Are you serious?" she asked, unable to hide her concern. "And you didn't think you should've told me this last night?"

"Damn," Dwight said. "No wonder you were so jumpy."

Harry glanced at Lacey. "I didn't tell you because there wasn't anything to do about it last night. I knew if I told you that you'd be up all night worrying."

She scoffed at him and crossed her arms. "Well, guess what? I was up all night worrying anyway," she snapped. "Why didn't you call the police?"

"I'm going to call the sheriff today," Harry answered.

Lacey jumped up from the table and reached for her cell phone that was charging on the kitchen counter. "I'm going to call him right now," she said, and she began a brisk walk toward the front door.

"Sis, can you wait a second," Dwight called after her. He sounded nervous.

"What is it?" she asked, pausing to look back at him.

"Don't call the sheriff yet," he said, sounding embarrassed.

Lacey took a step back toward him. "Why not?" she asked, though she was afraid she already knew the answer.

"Well...I uh—I kinda had a run in with the sheriff when I arrived into town," he said. "If you're gonna call him, please give me a chance to leave first. He said he wanted me to leave town or he was gonna arrest me."

"Arrest you for what?" she asked, sounding more agitated than concerned.

Dwight swallowed and pushed his plate back a bit. "Well, I uh…" he paused. "I uh…I kinda got caught with something illegal yesterday."

Lacey took another step toward him. "You got caught with *what*?" she asked.

He closed his eyes and Harry sensed he wanted to just disappear. "It was just a little coke," he answered. "I got pulled over and I was searched. The sheriff took it and told me to get out of his county or he'd have me arrested."

Harry took a deep breath through his nose and shook his head. "Well, that's just great," he grumbled. "Some things never change."

Lacey glared at her husband and then turned a similar look to her brother. "Dwight, I thought you were done with all that?"

He looked at his sister and seemed genuinely ashamed. "I'm really doing a lot better," he said, and he looked away from her.

Harry rubbed his chin and looked to his wife. "Well, what do you want me to do?" he asked.

She sighed. "Call the sheriff and tell him what you found. Just remind him to go talk to those brothers and let him know if they keep showing up here, we can't be held responsible for anything bad that happens to them."

Harry nodded and stood from the table. "I'm going to get dressed and start my first day at work," he said. "We'll talk about this more later."

When Harry was gone from the room, Lacey sat down at the table. "I've got to start work today too," she said. "Dwight, you're welcome to stay around here but please do me a favor and stay out of trouble?"

She reached a hand across the table and Dwight took it. "I promise," he said. "And thanks for always looking out for me."

"Someone has to," Lacey said, and then she too went upstairs to get dressed.

***

Once everyone was gone, Dwight returned to the barn to check on his bike. He was relieved to find that it was exactly where he'd left it, seemingly untouched. The motorcycle had started running rough somewhere between Baton Rouge and the Mississippi state line. Dwight suspected it was a fouled plug, so he rummaged in the bike saddlebag for the tools needed to change it. He'd just worked the plug free when suddenly, something banged loudly against the back wall of the barn. The sound was abrupt and loud enough that it startled Dwight to the point he fell backward.

"Wh-Who is there?" he called out.

He quickly regained his footing and dusted himself off. "Who is out there?" he asked again.

No answer, but a terrible stench began to fill his nostrils. It smelled of decaying flesh.

Clearly, the sound originated from the exterior of the barn. Dwight squinted as he tried to spot movement between the cracks of the boards that made up the rear wall. Almost immediately he noticed a dark figure moving on the other side of the wall.

"Hey…who is out there?" he called out.

Still no answer.

Dwight felt an uneasiness creeping up his spine and without considering the matter further, he again reached for the bike saddlebag. He pulled a handgun from inside and quietly made his way outside the barn. Dwight walked softly and rounded the front corner with the gun held out in front of him. Part of him was disappointed that there was nothing there to greet him…and part of him was relieved. With his heart rate increasing, he made his way toward the next corner—the corner that would bring him to the back of the barn. He took a deep breath when he reached it, and then quickly darted around it, prepared to confront whatever was lurking there.

There was no one there but Dwight did notice something odd on the sandy ground. He knelt and eyed what appeared to be a large human footprint. The print was enormous, so large that he estimated the foot had to be at least twenty inches long—maybe longer. Dwight immediately thought back to what Harry had said about the large handprints on the outside of the house. Instantly, his head was on a swivel and he scanned all directions for something watching him. He saw nothing, and just as he was beginning to feel safe again, he heard a loud rustling in the nearby trees.

Dwight stood and barely caught sight of a large figure disappearing into the shadows. It was standing upright and walked like a man. At first, he thought it *was* a man but then he noticed it seemed to be covered in hair.

"Hey! Stop!" he shouted.

Before he even realized what he was doing, Dwight chased after the mysterious retreating figure. The gun in his hands made him feel secure and part of him also felt that he owed it to his sister and Harry to find out who—or what—had been scaring Alice the night before.

Once he was into the woods, he lost sight of the giant he was chasing, but he could still hear it crashing through the trees ahead of him. It seemed that the man—if that's what it was—was moving at a high rate of speed. As fast as he ran, Dwight was losing ground. He told himself that he wouldn't stop, at least not until he could no longer hear the thing running away from him. He'd do everything he could to catch it and only when there was no sound left to guide him would he stop. His side began to ache, and he began to remember just how out of shape he was. Despite the pain, he pushed onward. Just as Dwight was beginning to think he'd lost the thing he was chasing, his foot caught a large root protruding from the ground. He hurtled forward and lost his grip on the gun in the process. When he struck the ground, he felt his head hit something hard, and unforgiving—probably a rock. And then, the world turned black and silent.

CHAPTER 8

Despite everything that had happened, Harry's first day at his new job had been very uneventful and bland. Uneventful and bland were a welcome change, one that he fully embraced. Baker County High School was a much smaller school than what he'd been used to, but again, this was a welcome change. A smaller school meant fewer students. Everyone there knew everyone else. That sort of comradery among the student body made his job much easier as the same principle seemed to work with the faculty as well.

The day had been a long one, and as soon as Harry returned home, something felt off. He couldn't put his finger on it and there was no logical explanation to explain why he felt the way he did, but nevertheless, the feeling existed. With a nagging reluctance, he exited the car and made his way up the steps leading to the front porch. When he reached the door, Harry paused and set his gaze over the meadow and ultimately to the edge of the woods. He wasn't sure what he was looking for, but he suddenly felt as if he was being watched. The bad feeling ratcheted up.

"I'm home," he announced as he trudged through the front door.

"Good, we're in the kitchen," Lacey called out to him.

There was something about her tone that didn't sit well with him. As soon as he rounded the corner and caught sight of his wife and daughter, he realized there was no longer a *feeling* telling him something was wrong. The expressions of sadness and concern across the faces of the two most important ladies in his life made it all a harsh reality.

"What happened?" he asked, pausing in the doorway.

"It's Dwight," Lacey said, her voice quaking slightly. "He's gone."

Harry sighed and crossed his arms. He knew that he would now have to tread lightly.

"Honey, Dwight didn't seem real comfortable here...especially since he'd already had a run-in with the sheriff. You can't blame him for moving on—"

"What?" she asked, cutting in suddenly. "I don't think you understand. I don't think he left...at least not on his own terms. I believe he was taken."

The statement took him by surprise. "*Taken?*" he said. "Why do you think that?"

"Because his bike is still out in the barn—along with his other belongings. His wallet is in the saddlebag," she added. "There's no way he'd leave that behind."

Harry looked away and considered what she'd said. He scratched the back of his head and then said, "Do you think he was into some sort of trouble that he didn't tell us about?"

Lacey closed her eyes and seemed to be doing her best to fight off the urge to cry. "It crossed my mind," she answered in a voice just above a whisper.

"I think we should call the police," Alice said suddenly. Harry had almost forgotten she was there. He looked to Lacey again.

"I think she's right," he said. "Something bad could've happened to him and we need to alert the authorities."

Lacey frowned. "You heard what he said...the sheriff told him to get out of town. If we call him and then Dwight turns up..."

"That doesn't matter now," Harry said, heading for the door. "I'm going outside and making the call."

Half an hour later, Sheriff Travis Horne arrived at their home for the second time in as many days. Harry thought he looked tired when he climbed from the patrol car. When he reached the top of the steps, he offered a forced smile.

"Okay," he said as Harry met him on the porch. "So, Lacey's brother is missing? You didn't tell me your brother-in-law was here too."

Harry rubbed the back of his neck and shifted his weight from one foot to the other. "Well, when you were here yesterday, he wasn't."

The sheriff eyed him curiously. "Okay...so he showed up after I left and now he's gone?"

"That's exactly right," Harry answered. "All of his belongings are still here, but he is not."

"I see," Sheriff Horne said. There was a bit of skepticism in his tone. "Did he show up here unexpectedly?"

Harry nodded.

"Then what's to stop him from leaving just as unexpectedly?"

"He left his bike," Harry explained. "He left his money and a bag of clothes. It doesn't make any sense."

"I see," the sheriff said, and he sighed. "Well, where is his stuff at?"

Harry set his gaze across the meadow to where the old red barn loomed. "In there," he said. As he looked back to the sheriff, he said, "Before we go over there, I guess I should mention that I think you had a run-in with my brother-in-law yesterday. It's my understanding you told him to leave town."

Sheriff Horne cocked his head slightly to the right and his eyes moved toward the wooden planks he was standing on. He seemed to be replaying the previous day's events in his head, searching for the moment Harry was referring to. "Ah yes," he said quickly. "I do remember running into a guy on a bike—a drifter…" he paused and locked eyes with Harry. "*That* guy was your brother-in-law?"

Harry inhaled through his nose and nodded. "Yeah…his name is Dwight. So, you remember him?"

The sheriff chuckled. "Yeah, I remember him…it's not every day I come across some guy with a tiny bag of cocaine in his pocket. That just don't happen in Baker County. I told him to get his ass out of my town and if I saw him again, I'd lock him up."

Harry noticed that Sheriff Horne's voice was rising slightly, and he became fearful that Lacey would hear the conversation and come outside. Though Dwight was a screw-up and worthless in Harry's opinion, the worthless screw-up was still Lacey's little brother. She was fiercely protective of him.

"Let's go check the barn out," he said, trying to lead the sheriff away from the house.

As they walked across the meadow, he said, "I appreciate you cutting him a break yesterday. Dwight is an idiot, but he's harmless."

"He may be harmless, but any guy bringing drugs into my county isn't welcome here, Harry. I meant what I told him yesterday and if we find him, I'm gonna lock him up," Sheriff Horne said.

"I understand," Harry replied. "At this point, it would probably do him some good. I just hope he's alright."

They arrived at the barn and the sheriff immediately made his way toward the bike. He began searching the saddlebags and went through Dwight's wallet. After that, he unzipped a small camouflage duffel bag and studied its contents. Inside the bag was change of clothes, a pack of cigarettes, some personal hygiene products, and a pornographic magazine.

"There's nothing here to suggest he was in any kind of trouble," Sheriff Horne said.

"Well, that's good, right?" Harry asked.

The sheriff returned the contents into the bag and zipped it back up. "Well, it's not bad," he said. "But it still doesn't rule out someone came and got him. It's still possible that your brother-in-law pissed off the wrong people and was on the run because of it."

Harry pushed his hands into the pockets of his slacks and began to accept the real possibility that Dwight could be gone for good. As he considered this, Sheriff Horne moved past him and to the exterior of the barn. With Harry out of view, he began to frantically examine the ground around him for clues. It didn't take long to find what he was looking for. The footprint was nearly two feet in length and Sheriff Horne knew all too well what it was. He quickly used his boot to erase it from the earth and he did the same with three other prints he found.

"Find anything?" Harry called out from behind him.

He'd snuck up on him, and it startled him. He did a good job of hiding it. "Nah, there's nothing," he answered, turning to look at him, his hands on his hips. "At this point, I think the best thing to do is to give it a day and see if he comes back. I'll have my deputies keeping an eye for him, but if I were a betting man, I'd bet my paycheck he comes knocking on your door real soon, probably from a bender he's having right now with someone."

The two men walked back to the house and Harry was dismayed to find Lacey standing on the porch waiting for them. Sheriff Horne looked over at him nervously and it was apparent he hadn't forgotten the confrontation from the day before.

"Hello, Sheriff," she said as they drew near.

Sheriff Horne removed his hat and smiled. "Good afternoon, Mrs. Schrader," he replied. "I want you to know I'm gonna have all my men looking for your brother. If he's still here in the county, we'll find him."

Lacey nodded and appeared grateful. "Thank you," she said. "I really appreciate it."

"It's no problem, ma'am," he said, and he turned to Harry. "Mr. Schrader, give me a call if you find out anything or if he shows back up."

"Will do," Harry answered, and the two men shook hands.

Just as Sheriff Horne was about to get into his car, Lacey called after him.

"Did you talk to those Conner brothers?" she asked.

The sheriff paused and leaned onto the roof of his patrol car. "I sure did," he replied. "Gave them a good talking to, but you should know that they both adamantly deny that they've recently been on this property."

"And you believe them?" she snapped.

The sheriff considered the question and then answered, "Yeah...I think I do, actually. Those boys have been in trouble enough to know when it's safe to lie and when it's safe to tell the truth. I think they have sense enough to know that what I was confronting them about wasn't a serious enough offense to lie about."

Lacey nodded. Harry thought she was done when suddenly she opened her mouth to speak again. "And you're sure there isn't anything you want to tell us about the previous owners of this house?"

Sheriff Horne smirked and ran a finger over his mustache. "This again?" he asked, somewhat annoyed. "Mrs. Schrader, I told you what I knew about the previous owners. Where is this coming from?"

Lacey crossed her arms and took a deep breath. She seemed to be struggling with what to say next. "I met an old man at the grocery store," she began.

"Say no more," Sheriff Horne interrupted, screwing up his face in disgust. "This guy was older than dirt and wore a baseball cap? Seemed a little cuckoo?"

Lacey looked to her husband and then back to the sheriff. "Yeah...sounds like you know him."

"Everyone in Dunn knows him," he answered. "That old man is the town crazy and you should stay away from him. You start listening to him and you're never gonna get any sleep. All he talks about is doom and gloom everywhere he goes. Take my advice and steer clear of him."

"I see," she replied. "Okay...I'll keep that in mind."

Without another word, Lacey turned and went back into the house.

"I'm getting the feeling that your wife can't stand me," Sheriff Horne said, glaring at Harry.

"Yeah, you picked up on that?" Harry asked. "That police training has served you well."

Sheriff Horne smirked, his mustache slanting to one side. "We'll be in touch, Mr. Schrader."

CHAPTER 9

Harry wanted to go and search the woods for Dwight, but Lacey wouldn't hear it. Part of her *did* want his help, but then another large part—the part that resented his affair—did not. Though she hadn't told him, Lacey was beginning to accept the real possibility that she and Harry would not be together for very much longer. She loved him, true enough, but what sort of example was she setting for their daughter Alice? Surely the young girl had noticed her father sneaking around and taking phone calls in private.

The next morning, after Harry had left for work, Lacey decided she'd go and do a bit of investigating of her own. Once Alice caught the bus to school, she pulled on boots and took a walk out to the barn. Once inside, she rummaged through Dwight's belongings, looking for any sort of clue regarding his disappearance. Just as Harry and Sheriff Horne had experience before her, she came up empty-handed and began to feel more frustrated than ever.

She began to move beyond Dwight's things and toward a darker, more obscure area of the barn. There was an old tarpaulin covering something in the corner and—with great anxiety and reluctance—she jerked it free. What she uncovered was several cardboard boxes covered in dust and cobwebs. Lacey curiously moved toward them and used the light on her cell phone to provide enough illumination for inspection. It seemed that there were all sorts of documents that had belonged to the previous owners. There were tax records, pay stubs, and check registers.

Lacey thought it odd that documents with so much personal information would be left inside of a fairly unsecured barn. She was grateful, however, that finally she had names to go with the mystery regarding the disappearance of the previous owners. They were the Billings—Ronald and Sara Billings. She took one of the registers and shoved it into the back pocket of her jeans. She'd come back to it later when she had a chance to dig up some information on the Billings. She rummaged a bit more through the boxes but found nothing else of significance.

Once satisfied that there was nothing more to be explored inside the barn, she ventured outside of it. She began to carefully and meticulously examine the ground for clues. Specifically, she searched for prints. There was no shortage of them to be found, however, there was also no way to differentiate between the prints of Harry, Sheriff Horne, and Dwight. Lacey made her way to the rear of the barn and again there were prints, but the same troublesome quandary remained. Determined to keep looking, she began to move away from the barn and toward the shadows of the looming trees that led into the forest. It was there that things began to get interesting.

There were more prints, but some of the prints, she noticed, looked very much like a human foot. However, the strange thing was that the footprints were nearly two feet in length. Lacey knelt for a closer look to make sure her eyes were not deceiving her. A cool breeze rolled out of the forest, blowing her blonde hair wildly around her head in the process. She felt a chill run up her spine and suddenly had an unsettling feeling that someone was watching her. The dogged determination to find Dwight overpowered her urge to flee and she kept looking. Soon after she began to notice shoeprints and, despite the voice in her head telling her to be cautiously optimistic, she swore they looked like they were made by the boots Dwight routinely wore. All the prints seemed to suggest what Lacey already knew…her brother had ventured into the forest.

It took a great deal of restraint to keep from going into the dense foliage in search of Dwight. It wasn't so much the fear of something happening to her as it was the possibility that Alice would come home with her mother nowhere to be found. Instead, with the Billings' check register still in her back pocket, Lacey decided to drive over to the Dunn Public Library to see what she could dig up on their mysterious disappearances. Her search began in the periodical section and, though it took a bit longer than she'd originally anticipated, she finally found an article that referenced what she was looking for. There was little in the way of an explanation regarding the Billings' disappearance. The newspaper merely reported what had happened and included a brief statement by Sheriff Travis in which he suggested the Billings had probably left town. Lacey began to read:

The disappearance of Ronald and Sara Billings has many Dunn residents scratching their heads and wondering why the local couple would leave town without taking any of their belongings with them. Both were active parishioners of Dunn Methodist Church and were well-liked throughout the community. "It's a mystery," stated Sheriff Travis Horne. "At this time, we've got no evidence to suggest foul play. I'm sure they had their own reasons for leaving but our department has no reason to waste resources investigating the matter any further. As far as I'm concerned, this case is closed."

The Billings had no other family to speak of and an administrator is expected to be appointed by the court on Friday to begin the process of handling the estate and any debts the Billings potentially left behind. When pressed further about the possibility that something could have happened to the missing couple, Sheriff Horne persisted that the woods behind their home had been searched using dogs and that everything in their home had been combed through for clues.

"They left town...end of story," the sheriff concluded.

Meanwhile, the people of Dunn and the surrounding areas of Baker County will move forward with plans for the annual Fall Festival in the town square. If anyone has any information regarding the disappearance of Ronald and Sara Billings, please contact the Baker County Sheriff's Department.

When Lacey finished reading the story, she reread it once more just to make sure she wasn't missing anything. It was utterly strange to her that the people of Dunn seemed to be willing to accept the sheriff's story without questioning it further. This was reinforced by the fact that she could find no more references to the Billings' disappearance in any later newspapers. They were all but forgotten.

Lacey decided that it wasn't good enough to stop there. She dug deeper and went back further in time where, much to her surprise, she found more instances of people vanishing from Baker County, just outside of Dunn. Another article, six years prior to the Billing's disappearance read:

Arnold Henderson disappeared from his home without a trace a week ago and no one seems to have any information regarding his whereabouts. The Baker County Sheriff's Department is currently investigating the disappearance but have so far turned up nothing. Sheriff Travis Horne encourages the public to contact his department if anyone knows anything concerning Mr. Henderson's disappearance.

"This is a small town and we're all a close-knit community," Horne said. *"If something sinister happened to Mr. Henderson, I'm sure we'd have turned up something by now. He had not lived here for very long and it's very possible that he simply grew tired of our great county and left."*

More alarming, the disappearances all seemed to originate in the same vicinity and all within a twenty-mile radius of the home she and Harry had just purchased. Desperate for more answers, Lacey made copies of several of the articles and set out for a new destination.

The old man was exactly where she thought he'd be. He was seated on the bench in front of the grocery store. He wore the same red baseball cap that adorned his head the first night she'd met him. He wore blue overalls with a gray T-shirt under them and dirty brown boots that looked as if they could be close to the same age as the man himself. Lacey pulled the car to a halt in one of the parking spots at the back of the lot. She sat there for a few moments trying to convince herself to approach him. There was something unsettling about him...something she couldn't quite put her finger on. Despite that fact, Lacey knew if she wanted more answers, he would probably be the most likely avenue for her to get them. She took a deep breath and exited the vehicle.

The old man saw her approaching and he smiled widely, as if he'd known all along she would eventually come and see him. Lacey smiled back at him and politely waved.

"Good to see you again," he said with a chuckle.

"You too," she said, and her pace slowed. It was as if something in her subconsciousness tried to talk her into turning around.

The old man seemed to notice her uneasiness and he looked away, as if embarrassed. "I suppose I should apologize for what happened the other night," he said. "I didn't mean to scare you."

Lacey sighed and suddenly felt a bit shameful. *Had she overreacted that night?*

"There is no need for an apology," she said, waving him off. "I'm sorry about the way I acted."

She paused and raked her fingers through her blonde hair. "I was hoping you'd take a few minutes to answer a few questions I have," she said sheepishly.

The old man cocked his head to the side stared, his gray eyes piercing through her. "I take it you're beginning to understand the grave danger you're in?"

Lacey felt a chill run up her spine and she nodded slowly. "I think I'm beginning to, yes," she replied. "Can you tell me what is going on?"

"Yes," he answered. He paused and looked around him as if he was trying to make sure no one was listening. "But are you sure you're ready to hear it?"

Lacey felt her heart rate increase. "I'm ready," she said, trying to sound confident.

It was obvious by the expression on the old man's face that he could see she was anything but. "Alright," he said after mulling it over for a minute. "I'll tell you what you want to know, but I have one request."

She looked at him, puzzled. "Alright," she said. "Name it."

Again, the old man looked around him if as he was worried someone was eavesdropping. "Take me away from this store," he said as his eyes met her again. "What we need to discuss must be done in private."

CHAPTER 10

Harry returned home at his usual time to find Lacey sitting in the porch swing. At first, he thought his wife was there waiting for him. Since their marriage was in trouble, he took this to be a good sign. Perhaps it would be the opportunity he was looking for to finally come clean with her. As he exited the car and began to mentally prepare himself for the difficult conversation, he caught sight of the old man seated next to her.

The two of them were smiling and chuckling about something when he approached. He could hear them talking but was unable to make any sense of it. When the man noticed his approach, he gave Harry a nod and a slight wave of his hand.

"This must be Mr. Schrader," the old man said, and he began to rise from where he was sitting.

"Yes, sir, it's me," he said. He shot Lacey a bewildered glance.

"This is Mr. Lowe," she said, and she reached over and grabbed the man's forearm. "No, please sit down, Mr. Lowe. There's no need to get up."

He waved her off and continued on until he was standing. "I'm an old man, not an invalid," he argued. "I'm Clifford Lowe," he added, turning to Harry. "My friends call me Cliff."

The two men shook hands.

"Nice to meet you, sir," Harry replied. "Lacey's right, no need to get up on my account, please sit back down."

"Oh, listen at the two of you," he groaned in return. "Just because I've got wrinkled skin doesn't mean standing has suddenly become a difficult chore for me."

Harry smiled and suddenly felt as if he'd insulted the man. "My apologies," he said. "I was just trying to be respectful."

Cliff eyed him, and his thin lips cracked into a smile. "So was I," he said, and he glanced toward Harry's car. "You've just arrived home and found a strange man sitting on the porch chatting it up with this beautiful bride of yours. I didn't want you to get the wrong idea."

The smile that was on Harry's face grew even wider. When he glanced at Lacey, he was amused to see that she was blushing. "Well," he said. "Now that you mention it, if you're not here to steal away my wife, may I ask what's brought on your visit?"

Cliff took in a deep breath and slowly craned his head around to look down at Lacey, still seated in the swing. "Well, should I tell him, my dear?"

Lacey sighed and bit her lip. She looked away from Cliff and up to her husband. "Yes, I want you to tell him everything that you just told me."

Harry looked at the both of them, a mixture of anxiety and curiosity etched on his face.

"Very well," Cliff said, returning his gaze to Harry. "Mr. Schrader, I know what happened to Mr. and Mrs. Billings."

Harry's eyes narrowed, and he slowly looked to Lacey, confused.

"I found out that's the name of the previous owners," she explained.

Harry raised his eyebrows and nodded. "I see," he said. "And you know what happened to them?" he asked Cliff.

The old man nodded, his watery eyes wide. "It was a wood ape," he stated matter-of-factly. "A rogue one. It pulled them into the forest and no doubt killed them both...probably ate most of them."

For a moment, Harry stood there emotionless. Eventually, he once again turned his attention to Lacey and seemed to be forcing himself not to smile. She wasn't smiling back.

Was this a joke? he wondered.

"Mr. Lowe, are you referring to Bigfoot?" he asked with a sigh.

Cliff nodded slowly, his eyes remaining wide. "That's *exactly* what I'm referring to," he answered. "And the Billings couple aren't the first ones that's disappeared from this house either."

Harry quickly surmised that the old man was serious and, whether the tale he'd begun was fact or not, he certainly believed it himself to be true.

"And you say the Bigfoot that's doing all this is rogue?"

"That's right," Cliff confirmed. "He's broken apart from a tribe of wood apes that live in the swamp lands along the state line. He's been on his own for probably three decades now."

"I see," Harry said, crossing his arms. He glanced over at Lacey, skepticism all over his face. "Do you believe all this?"

She nodded and stood from the porch swing. "Yes, I do," she replied. "I looked around the barn today and noticed some footprints near the wood line that were too large to be human. Then I went to the library to do a little digging and I found that there have been a lot of disappearances in Baker County over the past thirty years. Time after time it's been swept under the rug by the local law enforcement and it seems that the local citizens just let them do it."

"That's because they *do* let them do it," Cliff interjected. "The people of Dunn—and all of Baker County—are fully aware of the rogue wood ape that's developed a taste for human flesh."

Harry sighed and resisted the urge to roll his eyes. "That makes no sense," he grumbled, gesturing toward the forest. "If there is indeed a Sasquatch running around in these woods killing people, then it would stand to reason that someone would hunt it down and kill it."

Cliff chuckled, and it was his turn to resist the urge to roll his eyes. "Mr. Schrader, I don't think I have to explain to you just how elusive these beasts are," he said. "A lot of men have tried and failed to hunt it down. Some ventured off into the forest never to return."

Harry looked Cliff in the eyes and placed a friendly hand on the older man's shoulder. "Mr. Lowe," he began. "Yes, I'm very much aware of how elusive Bigfoot is. I don't think that's a coincidence either. The thing doesn't exist. It's a myth— folklore."

He caught a glimpse of Lacey eyeing him from behind Cliff. The look she gave him was one of disapproval.

"Okay…okay," he said, holding up his hands apologetically. "But I have to ask," he added to Cliff. "Have you ever seen this thing for yourself?"

The old man's eyebrows rose, and his mouth became a straight line. "Yes, I have," he said softly. "The thing tried to kill me back in '85. I just barely escaped with my life."

Harry's brow furrowed as he was suddenly intrigued. "Really?" he asked in wonder. "How did you get away?"

Cliff turned away from him and took a deep breath through his nose. His mind seemed to wander to a day long ago, though the details of that day were still etched clearly in his mind.

"I came across the wood ape in Sanderson Swamp. It's through there, on the other side of the forest," he said, pointing. "I was new around here and I knew nothing about a tribe of wood apes—as a matter of fact, I was a lot like you. I didn't believe in such a thing." He paused and turned back to look at Harry, his gray eyes piercing. "But hear me, Mr. Schrader, when I tell you that when a monster like that grabs you by the throat and begins to squeeze…well…" he paused again and shuddered.

Some of the skepticism began to leave him and Harry felt gooseflesh appear on his arms. "What did you do?"

Cliff shifted his weight and looked down at the boards below his feet. "I was losing consciousness and just as the world turned black, I jerked my hunting knife free and planted it firmly into the wood ape's right eye," he explained. He brought his head up quickly to look at Harry again. "The thing roared a nightmarish wail that turned my blood cold, but it released me. It retreated away into the forest in obvious agony. Of course, I wasted no time gathering myself up and getting the hell out of there."

Despite the strain their marriage was under, Lacey moved near Harry and put her arms around his waist. He sensed she was just as unsettled as he was, and he held her close. "You say this Bigfoot…it's rogue, and it's developed a taste for human flesh?" he asked.

Cliff nodded slowly. "Wood apes aren't naturally dangerous to humans," he said. "Avoiding humans has been an essential element to their survival. Having said that, they are meat-eaters, and when a member of their tribe is exiled…well, the beast has to eat however he can."

"And why exactly would one of them become exiled?" Lacey asked.

"Probably attacked a human," Cliff answered. "This wood ape's taste for human flesh is probably what got it kicked out of the tribe in the first place. They're a lot like humans, you know. There are lots of good people in this world…and then there are monsters that call themselves human."

"So, since this thing's been exiled," Harry said. "It's been forced to live closer to where people are, and since it's also acquired a taste for human meat, it's become perfectly content with that."

"That's right," Cliff replied.

"And the local law enforcement keeps this fact hidden?" he asked in disbelief.

Cliff swallowed, his Adam's apple bobbing as he considered the question. "They keep it quiet because they know there is nothing they can do," he explained. "They keep it quiet because the wood ape typically takes one or two folks a year—that seems to be enough to satisfy the thing's craving. It's usually out-of-towners that get taken because they just don't know any better."

Suddenly, Lacey released her arms from around Harry and moved in front of him where she could look him in the eyes.

"And now it has Dwight," she said somberly. "We have to do something."

Harry's eyes widened. "And just what do you suggest we do?" he asked.

"We need to look for him," she answered.

Harry sighed and cleared his throat. "Lacey, if this…" he paused, as he realized he had suddenly become a believer. "If this…Sasquatch has taken Dwight, then it's probably too late."

Lacey shook her head. "Maybe not," she snapped. "We talked about that before you got here. Mr. Lowe tells me that if it had already eaten, then Dwight could still be alive. It could be keeping him in its lair."

"You think it's saving him to—to eat him later?"

"I certainly hope so," she answered.

"It's very possible," Cliff said. "Mrs. Schrader tells me that the remains of a deer were found on your property two days ago. The wood ape may not be ready for his next meal yet…but there isn't much time."

Harry kept his eyes on Lacey. He could see that she was nowhere near accepting that Dwight was gone for good. If she believed her brother was still alive, he owed it to her to try and find him. He looked over at Cliff.

"Okay, I'll look for him, but you said yourself that no one can find these things," he grumbled. "Just where should I start?"

Cliff smiled mischievously. "Actually, I said that a lot of men have tried and failed to find them," he said. "I know exactly where the wood ape lives. I've been watching it for years, waiting for my opportunity."

"Your opportunity to what?" Harry asked curiously.

"To kill it," he answered. "I'm going with you and we'll find your brother-in-law together."

As the two men continued to discuss the matter, Lacey suddenly bolted off the porch. She began screaming.

"Lacey!" Harry called after her, confused about her odd behavior. He peered across the meadow in the direction where she was running, and it was then that he caught sight of what she was running toward. It was Dwight.

CHAPTER 11

Dwight was bloodied, bruised, and wearing nothing but his underwear. As Harry looked him over, he could see what appeared to be bite marks on parts of his body as well. When Lacey met him at the edge of the meadow, her brother collapsed into her arms.

"Dwight!" she screamed. "Oh my God…what happened to you?"

Harry had knelt beside her and out of the corner of his eye, he noticed Cliff was standing just behind him, peering with interest. Dwight was mumbling something that at first was incoherent. Lacey continued to say his name and ask him what had happened and where he had been. Dwight's mouth was moving but it was impossible to make out what he was saying.

"Be quiet," Harry snapped to Lacey. "He's trying to tell us something!"

Lacey immediately closed her mouth and for the first time, she seemed to notice her brother attempting to speak.

"It's still out there," Dwight said in a raspy voice just above a whisper. "It—it's out there and it's coming."

Harry stood up suddenly and peered into the forest. "We need to get him to a hospital."

It was true enough that Dwight needed medical attention. However, Harry's real motivation was the fear of Dwight's declaration.

"What is coming?" Lacey asked, somewhat hysterically. "Tell us what happened."

Dwight looked over at his sister and seemed to be fighting to remain conscious. He opened his mouth and moved his lips, but no words came out.

"Lacey," Harry said, placing a firm grip on his wife's shoulder. "We need to get him to a hospital...now."

She looked up at him, her lip trembling.

"We can get answers from him once we've gotten him some medical attention."

She nodded, and then gently placed her brother's arm around her neck so she could help him up. Harry grabbed his other arm and contributed to the effort. They gingerly helped him into Lacey's car and he fell across the backseat, collapsing from apparent exhaustion.

"You take care of him and I'll get Mr. Lowe home," Harry said. "I'll meet up with you once I drop him off."

Lacey nodded and, after retrieving Alice, raced away toward the hospital.

"Poor thing, I hope she is careful and doesn't have an accident," Cliff said as he watched the car disappear leaving nothing but a cloud of dust.

"Me too," Harry said, as he opened the driver's door of his own car.

Cliff climbed in and fastened his seat belt. As Harry cranked the vehicle, the old man asked, "So do you believe now?"

Harry nodded. "Yeah, I believe it now," he said. "He seemed pretty convinced it was still coming after him."

Cliff nodded and glared at him somberly. "He's right," he answered. "I don't know how your brother-in-law got away, but rest assured the wood ape will be back."

They reached the end of Isley Road and Cliff began to rattle off directions to his home. As it turned out, it wasn't very far from where the Schrader's lived. As they rumbled around a country road Cliff said, "I hope your wife is prepared because no one at the hospital will pay the story about the wood ape any mind when they're treating her brother."

"Didn't think they would," Harry answered, his eyes fixed on the road ahead. "How do you think they will handle it?"

"Oh, they'll take good care of him," Cliff replied. "And they will listen to what they're told. Hell, some of them will know good and well what happened to him, but I assure you none will engage in conversation about it anymore than they have to."

Clifford Lowe's home was an old ranch-style house that was in desperate need of a new coat of paint. The lawn and surrounding landscape had been neglected and there was a lot of clutter under the carport. It was apparent that Cliff was not much of a housekeeper.

"Were you surprised that Dwight was still alive?" Harry asked as the car came to a halt.

Cliff looked over at him and his eyes answered the question before he nodded. "Yep, I was," he said. "Wood apes are finicky eaters," he explained. "Maybe there was something about Dwight he didn't quite like. Sooner or later, he'd have probably gotten hungry enough but..." he paused. "I don't know. I just knew your wife was hopeful and I wanted her to hold on to it, no matter how slim her brother's chances were."

Harry nodded. "Thank you for that," he said. "She and I haven't been getting along very well lately. I'm not sure she would've opened up to me as she did to you."

Cliff stared at him sympathetically. "Well, I don't know what's going on between the two of you, but I hope it works out," he said. "She's a good woman and you seem to be a good man. That little girl of yours has some good parents. Sometimes it just doesn't work out but never lose sight of what's important."

"Never," Harry said, staring out the windshield. "Alice is what's most important." There was an awkward silence and Harry found himself wondering how he got to the place of discussing his marital problems with a stranger. Despite this fact, he felt the need to say more...to get it all off his chest. "She thinks I'm having an affair," he said bluntly.

Cliff nodded. "I see," he said quietly.

There was another moment where neither man said anything when finally, Harry said, "I'm not though."

Cliff smiled. "I hoped not," he replied. "But I wasn't about to ask. It's not any of my business."

Harry continued to stare out of the windshield. His mind seemed to be elsewhere.

"I have cancer," he said, almost in a dream state.

Cliff took a breath, surprised by the revelation. "I-I'm sorry," he stammered.

"Lacey doesn't know. I'm keeping it from her," Harry explained. "She's caught me on the phone a couple of times when I've been speaking with my doctor. I've tried to hide what's going on but the perception on her end has been that I'm having an affair."

"Look, it's obviously none of my business," Cliff said. "But why don't you just tell her what's really going on?"

Harry smiled awkwardly. "It's not that I don't want to," he said. "It's just that...I know when I do, things will be different. It will no longer just be my fight, it'll be hers too, and I don't want her to feel sorry for me. It's my job to be strong and supportive for her and Alice. I don't want to lose that."

Cliff reached over and grabbed Harry's forearm, squeezing slightly. "Don't let pride get in the way of what's important," he said. "True enough, your wife and daughter need you. I'd venture to guess that the man they have right now isn't really *you* anymore. Am I right?"

Harry considered the old man's wise words. He understood completely what he meant. It was true that he had been anything but himself since he'd received the cancer diagnosis. He'd become distant and secretive—a shell of the man he usually was.

"You're right," he conceded finally. "I'll tell her when we're no longer being hunted by Bigfoot," he added with a chuckle. "I think she can only handle one traumatic event at a time."

Cliff adjusted his cap and laughed. "Yeah, I think that would be wise," he said.

The older man got out of the car. Once he was standing outside, he leaned over and peered back in at Harry. "Come in," he said. "I've got something to show you."

Harry considered the request and thought of Lacey at the hospital with Dwight. As if reading his mind, Cliff said, "There is nothing you can do about that right now. What I've got to show you I think will be worth your while."

Unable to contain his curiosity, Harry exited the car and followed Cliff into the house. Once inside, Cliff flicked on the lights and Harry quickly determined that the interior of the house was just as bad—if not worse—than the exterior of the home. It did not appear that the house had been dusted or vacuumed in years and there were cobwebs in the corners of the ceiling.

"I'm not much of a housekeeper," Cliff said sheepishly. "Please ignore the clutter and follow me."

He led Harry down a narrow hallway and then into a room at the rear corner of the house. Harry heard him flip a switch and a fluorescent light sputtered to life above him. He then surveyed his surroundings in awe. Every wall in the room was covered in newspaper clippings, maps, and photographs. All the information around him was connected to Bigfoot sightings and disappearances of people all over the world. He noticed many grainy pictures of Bigfoot, some were the famous ones he was quite familiar with and some were more obscure and new to him.

"I guess now I see why you're not a good housekeeper," Harry muttered with mild amusement.

Cliff nodded and looked around the room, a bit of pride emanating from him. He walked toward one of the eight by ten photographs and pulled the thumbtack holding it in place free. He handed the picture to Harry and as he looked it over, his eyes widened with a mixture of excitement and horror. He looked over at Cliff.

"Is this…is this what I think it is?

"Yes," Cliff replied quickly. "That's the rogue wood ape of Baker County."

Harry studied the photo closely. The beast he was looking at appeared to be close to nine feet in height. It was broad and muscular in build, probably weighing at least 400 pounds. The body was covered in brown fur the color of dark chocolate. The hands were massive but were not much different from his own. Harry squinted as his eyes drifted to the beast's face. He took note that only one of the eyes was open and it gave off an aura of sinister rage. The other eye was scarred and seemed to be sealed shut.

"I'm responsible for that," Cliff said, noticing what Harry was looking at.

Harry looked up at him. "You're telling me that *this* is what took Dwight?"

Cliff nodded.

"And you're not afraid that it won't someday come for you?" Harry asked. "After all, you're the one that took its eye."

The old man smiled mischievously. "Oh, how I wish it would," he growled. "I would love to kill it and expose it for the entire world, so I could once and for all put this business of them being a myth to rest. One day…I will."

CHAPTER 12

As Harry prepared to head toward the hospital, Lacey called him and let him know that Dwight was, for the most part, fine but the hospital would be keeping him overnight for observation. She encouraged him to head home and she'd see him soon. With the image of the Sasquatch, or wood ape as Cliff called it, burned into his memory, it was all he thought about on the drive home.

When he arrived home, everything *seemed* normal, but when he entered the house, Harry discovered it was anything but. The place was ransacked. The couch and coffee table were turned over, pictures were knocked from the walls, and there were various books ripped from the shelves. A terrible stench hovered in the air. The sight in front of him was startling and Harry nearly retreated from the house at once. Instead, he somehow found the courage to venture further inside.

"Anyone in here?" he asked. He wasn't shouting, but his voice was firm and steady.

There was no response.

As he went along into each room, he reluctantly turned on the lights. Each time he did this, Harry mentally prepared himself to come face to face with the beast in Cliff's picture. When he entered into the kitchen and flipped the light switch, it was soon apparent where the intruder had entered. The back door was not just broken loose, it was completely torn from its hinges. The heavy wood now lay in the center of the kitchen floor and the coolness of the night drifted in from the outside. Suddenly, with the door open, Harry felt vulnerable and a chill ran up his spine.

Calm down, he told himself. *If the beast was still here, it would've gotten you by now...*

After retrieving a flashlight from the kitchen drawer, Harry rummaged around the barn until he found a couple of boards he could use to hold the door in place for the night. He worked quickly, doing his best to complete the task before Lacey and Alice returned home. It would be difficult enough keeping them calm when he had to explain what had happened without the house being in disarray too. Once the door was reinforced, he set about returning the furniture, pictures, and books back into their rightful places.

Harry wondered if there was some sort of method to the madness regarding the wood ape's behavior when it had entered the house. Had it expected to find them inside? Or did it purposely wait until they were gone to go inside and wreck the place? He hoped that it was the latter. Whatever its motive, it clearly wasn't going away. Harry considered everything Clifford Lowe had said about the beast's behavior, and the fact that this one in particular was a rogue—exiled from its tribe. Its hunger for human flesh was apparently back, and unfortunately the Schrader family had become the chosen target. It would be up to him to protect his family.

Half an hour after he'd returned the house into relative order, the front door swung open and Lacey, with a groggy Alice, had returned.

"Go upstairs and get into bed," Lacey told the girl. "You can get a shower in the morning."

Alice yawned, but made no protest and she began to ascend up the stairs that ultimately led to her bedroom.

"How's Dwight?" Harry asked, genuinely concerned.

"No change from what I told you on the phone," she answered. She yawned and was clearly tired too. "No broken bones, just lots of contusions and cuts. He was a bit dehydrated but there was nothing seriously wrong with him."

Harry nodded approvingly. "That's good," he said. "Did you get a chance to speak anymore with him about what happened?"

Lacey looked at him, her tired eyes showing fear. "Yeah," she said. "He told anyone that would listen what happened to him."

"And how did they take it?" Harry asked. He was truly interested to see if their reactions would line up with what Cliff had suggested they would be.

She crossed her arms and considered the question. He could see her replaying the interactions between Dwight and the medical staff in her head. "About like you'd expect," she said, shrugging. "They asked me about his mental state and they called the police."

Harry arched an eyebrow. "They called the police?"

She nodded. "Yes, a deputy came by and examined him. He asked me what happened, and I lied…I told him I didn't know. I explained he'd been missing for a little over 24 hours and that he'd stumbled out of the woods."

"I'm surprised Sheriff Horne didn't show up," Harry said.

"Well, I'm sure he knows by now," Lacey replied. "Anyway, the deputy seemed unconcerned, made a report and took off."

She moved past him and headed toward the kitchen.

"Wait," Harry called after her.

"Just a second," Lacey answered. "I'm thirsty."

Her pace never slowed, and Harry could only trail quickly after her. She stopped abruptly when she entered the kitchen, the boards over the back door immediately catching her attention.

"What happened here?" she asked, an obvious tone of worry in her voice.

Harry sighed and placed a hand on her shoulder. "We apparently had a visitor," he replied softly.

She whirled around at him. "What?" she snapped. "What visitor?"

Harry stared at her, unsure what to say for a moment. She knew exactly what visitor he was referring to. There was a long moment where neither of them said nothing.

"We have to get out of here," Lacey said finally, tears welling up in her eyes.

Harry looked at her, incredulously. "Go? Go where exactly?"

Her lips trembled, and her face contorted into a mixture of rage and fear. "I don't know," she said. "But we need to leave or we're going to die."

Harry shook his head. "It's late and Alice has school tomorrow," he said. "I'll stay up tonight and make sure it's safe."

It was obvious that she wanted to argue the matter further; however, the exhaustion she currently felt seemed to stifle it away. Instead, she nodded weakly and trudged upstairs to get a shower.

"Don't worry," Harry called after her. "Everything is going to be fine."

Lacey didn't reply, and he began to wonder if she was angry at him. He thought back to the discussion he'd had with Cliff and knew he'd have to come clean with her about his cancer very soon. In truth, he wished he could tell her immediately, but with everything else going on, it was just too much. Temporarily pushing the thoughts aside, he began to work out a plan on how he'd manage the night to ensure he'd keep his family safe.

Harry's first stop was to the utility room where his tools were kept. He grabbed a claw hammer and a box of nails then methodically moved from room to room, nailing each window shut. Logically, the exercise seemed useless as he was very aware that if the beast wanted to come into the house, it could simply break the windows. However, something about it made him feel more secure and he figured the sound of the hammering and bustling about would make Lacey feel a little more at ease too.

Once he was satisfied with his efforts, Harry set about making a pot of coffee. By his estimation, it was going to be a long night and he needed all the help he could muster to stay awake. As the coffee brewed and the pleasant aroma began to waft through the house, Harry trudged up the stairs and strolled into the bedroom where Lacey was already snoozing. Quietly, he rummaged around in the top of a closet until he found what he was looking for. He'd never been a gun person but recognized the need to have one for security purposes. Lacey, on the other hand, had grown up hunting and was much more acquainted with firearms than he. Now, with the small handgun clutched firmly in his hand, he had never been so glad to have the weapon available, though he wondered just how much damage it would do to the enormous wood ape he'd seen in the picture.

The coffee helped, but it fell very short of eliminating the heaviness in Harry's eyelids. It was a struggle to stay awake, and it seemed the only thing that truly perked him up was the hourly round he made throughout the house in search of the prowler. Part of the time he'd spent reading an eBook on his phone, but soon even that wasn't enough to stifle off the intense urge to sleep. The house was enveloped in complete darkness, but his eyes had plenty of time to adjust. A large part of him longed for the morning so that he could get a bit of rest as he'd already decided he would most certainly not be going to work. Then there was another part of him that desperately wanted the creature to show up so that he'd have the opportunity to end the ordeal once and for all.

The clock had ticked near 4:00 am and Harry had all but decided that the danger, at least for that particular night, had been avoided. The sun would begin to rise in a short while and then he'd finally be able to get the sleep his body desperately craved. As his mind drifted to thoughts of crawling into a warm bed and snoozing for a few hours, his eyelids grew more and more heavy. Before he realized what was happening, Harry was drifting off to sleep. He'd been dozing for less than ten minutes when a sound suddenly startled him awake. The boards on the front porch were creaking under the weight of something large moving across it and toward the door.

CHAPTER 13

Harry made a brisk but quiet walk to the foyer as the footsteps on the porch grew louder. He crouched low and his heart beat so loudly in his ears, he was genuinely fearful that whatever was on the other side of the door would be able to hear each and every thump. As he forced himself to peek outside, he looked just in time to notice a dark, shadowy figure quickly moving away from the door and ultimately disappearing around the corner. With his adrenaline racing, and every fiber of his being screaming at him to stay put, Harry found the courage to quickly open the door and take off in pursuit of what was undoubtedly the wood ape.

As he rounded the corner of the house, the stench of the beast filled his nostrils and was so strong he felt a wave of nausea overcome him. He did his best to hold the terrible feeling at bay but was also dismayed to find no sign of the wood ape ahead of him. Harry kept the gun firmly in the grip of his right hand, the barrel pointed ahead of him. Now afraid that he was going to miss his opportunity, Harry took off running and began scanning all around him for any sign of movement. It was only once he'd made it to the opposite side of the house that a frightening thought popped into his head.

The front door is still open, he realized.

Without another moment of hesitation, Harry again took off in a sprint back to the front of the house. The door was indeed still open, and he swiftly moved toward it, praying his error would not prove to be a tragic one. As he drew near the doorway, a blood-curdling scream pierced through the silence of the night. It was coming from upstairs and he knew immediately that it was Lacey. Harry's heart was pounding as he clumsily ascended the stairs, the hand holding the gun was shaking uncontrollably. The fear of coming face to face with the frightening beast would be nothing compared to the fear of finding his wife and daughter mauled to death.

When Harry reached the doorway, the same dark and shadowy figure he'd seen on the porch was now standing at the foot of his bed. The thing was breathing deeply, so deep that its shoulders moved up and down in a sadistic rhythm that reminded him of various monsters in horror movies he'd seen as a boy. Lacey was still screaming—screaming maniacally. The wood ape didn't even turn to look at Harry, its attention planted firmly on Lacey. It was clear to him that it meant to tear her to shreds right where she was. Harry raised the gun, his hand still trembling, and fired a shot into thing's back. It howled in fury, and immediately moved a large hairy paw toward the spot where it had been hit. The wood ape continued to make frantic howls and Harry couldn't tell if it was a reaction to pain or fury. His gut told him it was probably the latter. Just as he was about to fire off another shot, the beast darted for the window and crashed through it, disappearing into the darkness.

Lacey immediately rolled out of bed and threw her arms around Harry. He could feel her heart pounding hard against his chest and figured she could feel his as well. She continued to scream and sob. He could hear her muttering words in between but was unable to make out anything except a mention of Alice.

"Let's go check on Alice," he whispered to her, assuming that was what she was trying to say. "It's okay now, it's gone."

No sooner had they both stepped into the hallway, the sound of heavy footsteps on the front porch were heard again.

"Get Alice and call the sheriff," Harry said, pushing her toward their daughter's room.

With the gun still clutched tightly in both his hands, Harry quickly made his back toward the stairs, just in time to see the wood ape coming up to meet him. Again, Harry fired off a shot at the foul beast and it roared ferociously in protest. The wood ape retreated down the stairs but remained inside the house, moving in the direction of the kitchen. With a healthy dose of adrenaline pushing him onward, Harry continued the pursuit and as soon as he rounded the corner that would lead him into the kitchen, he fired another shot. It was his hope, of course, that he'd be able to put another bullet into the wood ape. The creature made no sound and Harry instead heard the sound of breaking glass and porcelain. He knew immediately that he'd hit the china cabinet on the far wall and it was a sickening indicator that he'd completely missed the wood ape. Suddenly, without any warning at all, the gun was knocked from his hand and sent flying across the kitchen. The dark shadow abruptly appeared in front of him and lunged at him. With little time to react, Harry grabbed a large knife from the block on the nearby counter and immediately plunged the blade into and through the large hand that was attempting to grab him.

This time, there was no doubt that the sound the wood ape made was indicative of pain. There was another howl, this one more high-pitched and pitiful. The beast grabbed at its wrist underneath the injured hand and examined the gruesome injury. Harry could only look on in terrified fascination as the wood ape seemed to make sense of what it was looking at and then proceeded to pull the knife free from its hand. There was another howl of pain followed by the knife clanging onto the wooden floor. Again, the beast retreated from the house and into the damp night air. Harry immediately retrieved the gun and resumed his pursuit yet again as he was desperate to put an end to the nightmare once and for all.

Once outside, there was a moment of panic as Harry was unable to find the fleeing wood ape. There was a full moon in the night sky and it illuminated the meadow before him. There was a low mist rolling across the high grass. Since he was unable to see the creature, Harry listened intently for any sound at all that would give him an idea of where it was at. Something caught his attention...the sound of someone talking? He listened harder and realized it was a woman's voice. She was talking low, but not quite low enough as he was able to quickly determine it was Lacey. Suddenly, he realized what was happening. The last thing he'd told her was to call the sheriff, but as he well knew, the cell service was next to nothing inside the house. Harry turned his gaze toward the pecan trees near the wood line and as expected, he saw the silhouette of a woman holding a phone to her head. A smaller silhouette was next to her that he determined was Alice.

With obvious concern for their safety, Harry began running in their direction. He wanted to yell at them—to beckon them to be quiet and come toward him but he kept quiet for fear of drawing attention to them instead. As he drew nearer, he realized that their backs were turned to him and they had no idea he was approaching. To his utter horror, Harry caught sight of the wood ape sprinting toward them from a location parallel to his own. They were, for all intents and purposes, in a foot race to determine the fate of Alice and Lacey. Now with nothing to lose, Harry shouted at them. He begged them to run to him as it quickly became frighteningly obvious there was no way he'd make it to them before the deranged beast.

His wife and daughter turned immediately when they heard him yell, but Lacey kept the phone to her head, continued speaking to whoever was on the other end, and remained right where she was. By the time she finally caught sight of the approaching wood ape, it was too late. The beast drew back and arm and struck her with enough force to send her at least fifteen feet away from where she'd started, her body crashing painfully into the damp earth. Alice screamed, unsure of how to react or what to do. Harry again shouted for his daughter to run toward him. He leveled the gun at the wood ape but was reluctant to fire as the creature was in close proximity to Alice. Ultimately, Harry was unable to bring himself to pull the trigger and it was a decision he'd soon regret as the wood ape scooped up the young girl and promptly disappeared into the shadows of the forest.

Alice screamed and begged for him to help her. Harry chased after them until he could no longer hear the screams of his terrified daughter. Blinded by tears, and on the verge of passing out, he finally stopped as he realized it was a useless endeavor. He knew that Lacey was lying on the ground, probably injured badly, and needed his help so with great difficulty, he forced himself to turn back. When he found her, she was unconscious and at first, he feared she was dead. A quick check of her pulse confirmed that she was indeed alive. There was an illumination in the grass near her right hand and Harry suddenly realized it was the cell phone. He picked it up to find that Sheriff Horne was on the line.

"Mrs. Schrader!" the sheriff said. He was saying it over and over.

"Horne," Harry said, his words steady and cold. "Lacey needs an ambulance and my daughter has been taken."

"Mr. Schrader," Sheriff Horne said. "I'm almost there…stay put."

"Horne," Harry said, seemingly ignoring the sheriff. "If anything happens to my daughter, I'm holding you personally responsible."

There was an awkward silence, but Harry could hear the man breathing. Without another word, he hung up the phone.

CHAPTER 14

When Sheriff Horne arrived, he found Harry kneeling beside Lacey underneath the large pecan tree at the edge of their property. The swirling blue lights originating from his patrol car flashed off and on over them a short distance away.

"The ambulance should be here any minute," he said as he jogged toward them. "How is she?"

Harry glanced up at him, obvious concern on his face. "She finally regained consciousness," he muttered, slight relief in his voice. "I'm pretty sure she has a concussion."

"Where's Alice?" Lacey asked as she noticed Sheriff Horne approaching. "Sheriff, where is my daughter?"

Harry shot Sheriff Horne a look that instructed him to keep quiet.

"I told you," he said, glancing back to his wife. "Alice is fine. I'm going to go get her so stop worrying."

Lacey's eyes darted from Harry to the sheriff suspiciously. "Help me up," she snapped. "I'm going with you."

"No, you're not," Harry replied, placing a firm hand on her shoulder. "Keep still."

Once he was convinced she was going to stay put, Harry rose and ushered Sheriff Horne out of earshot from Lacey.

"Sheriff, can I trust you to look after my wife?" he asked, his eyes were threatening and scared all at the same time.

Sheriff Horne stared at him, confused. "Of course, but you're gonna be right here with her."

Harry shook his head. "No, I've got to go and get my daughter," he answered.

Sheriff Horne sighed and placed his hands on his hips. "Why don't you let me handle that?" he asked, trying to sound sympathetic. "Let me and my deputies do a sweep of the woods here behind your house. If she's out there, we'll find her." He stepped toward the meadow and peered across it.

Harry's eyes narrowed. "Don't you want to know what happened here, Sheriff?" he asked sharply.

Sheriff Horne suddenly whirled around to look at him. The expression on his face was a mixture of embarrassment and uneasiness. He stared into Harry's eyes for a long moment before saying, "I'm sorry, Harry," he said softly. "I like you, really, I do...but it's chosen you and there is nothing I can do about that now."

Harry took a deep breath through his nose and marched toward the sheriff with purpose, his hands balled into fists. "You just sit on the sidelines and allow this to continue to happen year after year?" he growled. "What a cowardly way to deal with the problem."

Sheriff Horne looked away shamefully. "You think I haven't tried?" he asked. "Well, I have. We can't find the damn thing. I've only seen it once. No one in this county likes to talk about it and it seems that as long as the locals stay safe, they're content with sharing the land with..." he paused. "With *it*."

"I see," Harry snarled. "As long as it's outsiders getting killed, the problem can be tolerated."

"Something like that," Sheriff Horne conceded. "I'm not proud of it, but it's been a way of life for a long time now."

"And somehow all of the longtime residents of this county never get taken?" Harry asked in disbelief.

The sheriff shook his head and moved his eyes up toward the moon in the sky above. "Nope, and it's because everyone is familiar with it. They know what parts of the county it hunts and for the most part they avoid it. It only seems to take one—maybe two people a year. Once that happens, the people of this county know they're safe for a while again."

Harry looked away, clearly disgusted. There was much he wanted to say, but as he thought of Alice, he knew this wasn't the time.

"Sheriff, can I trust you to look after my wife?" he asked for the second time.

Sheriff Horne scowled at him. "Once again, yes you can," he snapped. "But you're gonna need my help if you're going after your girl. Wait until my deputy arrives and we will go together."

Harry shook his head and began walking away. "No thanks," he grumbled. "I think I'll go get help elsewhere."

Lacey suddenly called out after him. "Harry, please bring her back!"

"Don't worry," he said, pausing to look back at her. "Me and Alice will meet up with you at the hospital shortly."

He noticed the glazed look in her eyes and wasn't entirely sure that she was completely comprehended what was happening. This was further evidenced by the blank expression she gave him in reply to his last words.

"Harry, let me send a deputy to help you," the sheriff called after him. It was more of a plea than a suggestion. "I don't want to see your kid get hurt—I swear it."

"I don't want anyone from your department helping me," he answered.

Sheriff Horne had to refrain from chasing after him. "You can't do this alone! Where are you going to find someone to help you?"

Harry opened the door to his car and momentarily paused to look at him. "I'll get some help from the only person in this town that's been shooting me straight," he snapped. "Look after my wife, Sheriff."

Without another word, Harry got into the car and sped away into the light of dawn. Minutes later, he brought the vehicle to a sliding stop in a dirt driveway he'd been in only a short time earlier. He then raced across the yard and across the porch where he then began to pound the door loudly to awaken Clifford Lowe.

Suddenly, the wood-paneled door swung open and Cliff eyed him, blinking.

"I'm sorry," Harry said, unable to completely disguise the panic in his voice. "It's gotten Alice and I don't know who else to turn to."

"Say no more," Cliff said, and he gestured for Harry to come inside.

Harry complied, but was reluctant to do so. "I've got to go," he said. "You said you know where it lives...I just need you to give me some directions. Can you maybe draw a map?"

Cliff said nothing and instead walked away, disappearing into a darkened hallway. "Wait here," he said from somewhere within the veil of darkness. Harry had to resist the urge to chase after him. Moments later, the old man returned with a large pistol grasped tightly in his wiry fingers.

"Colt 45," he said, holding the weapon up proudly. "Been saving it for this occasion."

"Is that going to be enough?" Harry asked.

Cliff glanced down at the gun in his hand and then back to Harry. "It'll do the job," he said confidently. He briskly moved past him and began to rummage through a desk that sat against the wall in the living room. The top of the desk was much like every other surface inside the home…covered in clutter. After a minute or two, he turned around and held out a flashlight for Harry to take. He had one for himself as well.

"We've got a few more minutes before daybreak," Cliff said. "We'll need these at first."

Harry nodded and anxiously walked toward the door. As he opened it, Cliff barged past him and seemed just as eager to leave.

"There is a trail behind the house," he said, still walking. "Follow me and stay close. Don't get in front of me."

Harry nodded and did as he was instructed. The two men moved along the wood line behind the house until finally reaching a well-beaten path that led into the dense foliage. Cliff continued to move at a brisk pace but kept quiet. Harry seemed to sense that, though he was never told, keeping quiet was a necessity if they were going to have any success in their endeavor. Under the canopy of the forest, the flashlights were necessary to navigate across the uneven terrain. Soon, however, the rays of the morning sun began to penetrate the natural shroud above them to the point the lights were no longer needed.

After what seemed like almost half an hour of walking, suddenly and without any warning, Cliff stopped. It was all Harry could do to keep from running into him. He waited for some sort of explanation but after a minute he became impatient.

"What's wrong?" Harry whispered.

Cliff turned his head slowly to look back at him. "We're here," he whispered back. He waved his hand toward a grove of pine trees. For a moment, Harry saw nothing, but just as he was beginning to think the old man was hallucinating, the well-camouflaged home of the wood ape came into view.

CHAPTER 15

At first glance, there appeared to be nothing ahead of them except for a vast collection of pine trees with slender trucks stretched upward and disappearing into the darkened sky. The ground was blanketed with pine straw so think that there was little evidence of green grass to be found in all directions. When Harry caught sight of the wood ape's home, he wondered to himself how in the world Cliff had managed to find it. The only thing that had caught his eye had been the opening. It was a smaller hole than he'd imagined, but once he studied it closer, it was definitely large enough to allow the creature an easy avenue to come and go as it pleased. The opening angled upward very slightly. This created a minor incline in what otherwise seemed to be flat terrain ahead.

"There's a deep ditch that runs across there," Cliff pointed out. He'd been watching Harry try to work out the architecture in his head. "The monster placed god knows how many logs across that ditch and then piled pine straw on top of that."

Harry felt his heart rate climb as he stared at the creature's home, unblinking. "Is it in there?" he whispered.

"I'm fairly certain that it is," Cliff replied. The gun was clenched tightly in his right hand and Harry noticed a slight tremble.

"Then that mean's Alice is in there," Harry said, and he lurched forward. Cliff grabbed his arm, stopping him in his tracks. Harry whirled his head around to look at him. "What are you doing?" he snapped, pulling his arm away.

"If you just prance into that thing's home, it's going to rip you apart before you can even lay eyes on your girl. You're no good to her if you're dead," the old man explained.

Harry grunted in disgust. "Okay, then what do you suggest?" he grumbled. "And whatever you've got, you better make it fast!"

Cliff rubbed at the stubble on his chin and then adjusted his cap. "I'll distract it, and when it comes out, then you go inside and get your girl," he said.

Harry stepped toward him. "Distract it how?" he asked. "What are you going to do?"

"I have my ways," the old man replied. "You go over there," he added, pointing to the rear of the wood ape's hut. "When it comes out of there, you move fast."

It was obvious to Harry that Cliff had made the plan up on the fly and as weak as it was, for the time being, it was all he had.

If there was any chance of getting Alice back alive, the time to act was now, not later.

"What if it comes for you?" he asked, unable to hide his concern for the older man.

Cliff smiled widely. "I hope it does," he answered, holding up the gun. "I told you, I've been waiting for this occasion for quite a while."

Harry sighed, and though he wanted to say more—to ask more questions—he instead moved cautiously toward the rear of the wood ape's home. As he drew nearer, the disgusting smell of the animal crept into his nostrils. It smelled like a combination of decaying flesh, body odor, and wet dog all wrapped into one terrible concoction of sickening sensory overload. The smell was intense enough that Harry felt as if he'd throw up. Somehow the thought of losing Alice quelled the sensation and his focus returned to the job at hand. He found a spot behind a pine tree— one of the widest ones in the vicinity. It still wasn't anywhere close to concealing him completely, but it would have to do. Harry then began looking intensely for Cliff and began to feel a sense of panic when he was unable to locate the old man.

Had he abandoned him?

Harry was almost certain that Cliff would do no such thing. There was an unsettling amount of glee in the old man's eyes when the prospect of potentially killing the beast came to fruition. In fact, Harry was having a hard time deciding if the old man's willingness to help him was due to his wanting to help Alice, or if it had more to do with his decades-long quest to destroy the wood ape that he'd become obsessed with.

Suddenly, a sinister growl rumbled through the trees. It was a despicable sound that made Harry's skin crawl and for a moment, he considered fleeing. The sound stopped for a moment, and then continued again. Harry again scanned his surroundings for any sign of Cliff when finally, he spotted him. He was leaned against another tree, not far from where he'd left him. It was then that Harry realized the other-worldly growling was originating from him. The old man continued the strange ritual for a few minutes when suddenly, the desired results were achieved.

Out of the opening at the front of the hut, the wood ape emerged. Its dark fur was matted and filthy with something sticky. Harry wondered if it was blood but pushed the awful thought aside. The creature stood over eight feet tall and its shoulders were nearly half as wide as the thing's height. It was a hulking monster and as it turned its large ape-like head in search of where the growling had been originating, Harry caught a glimpse of missing eye—the one Clifford Lowe had claimed many years before.

Harry could only look on helplessly as the hulking figure lumbered slowly toward Cliff. The old man remained where he was but was now deadly quiet. The beast towered over Cliff as it drew nearer, but the best Harry could tell, it had not yet spotted him. Without considering the matter any further, he bolted around the far side of the wood ape's home and quickly slid downward into the opening. The slope was much steeper than he anticipated, but it was well-traveled. The soil was packed so tightly that it felt like cement, and Harry was thankful that he hadn't landed on it any harder than he had.

Once he'd reached the bottom and his eyes adjusted to the darkness, Harry marveled at the size of the interior of the hut. The ceiling was high—at least as high as the wood ape was tall. He estimated that each of the four walls measured approximately twenty feet in length. As he moved deeper into the foreign structure, his foot caught something that he at first believed was a rock. Harry paused and knelt for a closer look. To his horror, the strange object wasn't a rock at all. It was a human skull. As he continued to peer at the ground around his feet, he noticed other skulls, and other bones that he quickly determined were human.

A chill ran up his spine and Harry felt perspiration form cold on his forehead. For the briefest moment, he forgot why he was there and considered fleeing. The terror he felt was so overwhelming it was impossible to ignore. The only thing that seemed to pull his attention away from the collection of bones was the stench he'd suddenly become all too familiar with. As bad as it was, in a way he was thankful for it as it seemed to return his attention to why he was there in the first place.

Alice.

It didn't take him long to find her. She was lying against the very back wall of the structure on top of a pile of clothes. Harry immediately recognized the clothes…they belonged to Dwight. He knelt and gently placed a hand on his daughter's shoulder. He shook her gingerly. Her body felt cool, and lifeless. There was a painful lump forming in the base of his throat and working its way upward as every second ticked by where Alice was non-responsive.

Just as he was beginning to lose hope, he heard it—the slightest gasp for breath. With his hope restored, Harry pulled his daughter upward so that she was sitting up, her back against his chest.

"Alice," he whispered frantically. "Alice, can you hear me?"

The small girl coughed and let out a tiny moan. "Daddy?" she asked, her voice frail.

Harry felt a smile spread across his face and resisted the urge to cry just as a gunshot thundered loudly from outside. "Thank God," he whispered. He quickly scooped the girl up and turned to make his retreat. They'd only made it halfway toward the slope when something came rolling down it. The object came to rest in front of Harry's feet and as he stared down at it, he struggled to believe what he was actually looking at. His heart rate kicked up another notch and he felt faint. The eyes looking up at him were open wide with terror—the mouth a straight line. Harry was looking at the decapitated head of Clifford Lowe.

CHAPTER 16

Thankfully, Alice was much too groggy and disoriented to know what was happening. Harry took a step back from the head and closed his eyes, willing himself not to pass out. Part of him was filled with terror and fear as he knew full well what was responsible for such a terrifying end to Cliff's life. Another part of him was filled with sadness and grief. Cliff didn't deserve what had happened to him and as the sadness continued to well up inside him, Harry forced himself to turn the emotions into pure unbridled rage. He felt his jaw tighten as he pulled Alice even closer to his body. Though the situation seemed dire, Harry was nowhere near giving up.

His eye caught movement near the slope that led to his freedom—to life. A shadow danced over the packed soil and several small pebbles rolled down across it. Harry took a deep breath and stepped backward as he readied himself for the inevitable confrontation. As expected, the wood ape came into view, but it stumbled and seemed injured. Though Harry was unable to tell for sure due to the beast's thick coat of hair, he suspected that the gunshot Cliff had managed to get off reached its intended target. As soon as the wood ape spotted him with Alice clutched in his arms, the creature growled menacingly and showed him its teeth. The fangs were like daggers, and much longer than what he'd imagined. They were brown, obviously stained from blood.

If the beast's sheer appearance wasn't frightening enough, the headless body being dragged behind it did more than enough to complete the effort. The wood ape took a step toward him, releasing the ankle of Clifford Lowe's corpse as it moved. Harry noticed the dark sheen of blood pooling up around the remains of Cliff and in his mind's eye, he pictured a similar fate for himself. His thoughts drifted toward Alice, still held tightly in his arms. He refused to even consider the same sort of ending for her and decided he'd sacrifice himself if necessary to save her life. His body was infected with cancer, and it was likely his life would be cut short anyway. Suddenly, it occurred to him that maybe that was why he'd been cursed with the disease in the first place—for the very moment that now stared him right in the face.

Harry stepped back to put more distance between himself and the wood ape. The monster eyed him curiously, but this time remained motionless. Keeping his eyes on the beast, Harry knelt and gently placed his unconscious daughter on the dirt floor. He slowly stood back up and walked in front of her.

"I—I don't know if you can understand me," he stammered. "But I'm begging you not to hurt my daughter."

The wood ape cocked its head slightly and moved the good eye from Harry, to Alice, and then back again.

Harry stretched out his arms on either side of him and held his hands out to show that he meant no harm. "Take me," he said, almost pleading. "Take me and let my daughter go."

For a long moment, the creature stared at him, breathing hard. There was a stern look upon its face and though it seemed to understand what Harry was suggesting, there was no empathy to be found in its expression. The wood ape walked cautiously to him and when it was within arms-length, it suddenly reached out and grabbed Harry by the throat.

Harry reached for the clawed fingers that wrapped around his neck and tried to pry them free with all his might. The fingers would not budge. He stared at the beast's good eye and it stared right back. The wood ape pulled Harry close to its face and began sniffing him. Harry closed his eyes and awaited the moment the creature would grow tired of toying with him and end his life once and for all. He just hoped it would be quick and painless. If it would save Alice's life, it would all be worth it.

The wood ape seemed to spend a great deal of time sniffing at Harry's mouth. His breathing was fast and panicked. There was no way he could control it. After almost a full minute of doing this, the creature eventually made a sour face.

It smells my cancer, he thought, astonished. *It smells my disease...*

The wood ape scowled and casually tossed him aside. He landed painfully on the ground right next to the headless corpse of Cliff Lowe. Almost immediately, he noticed that the old man still had the revolver clutched tightly in his hand. Harry shot a quick glance back to the wood ape and saw that the beast was moving toward Alice, its back turned to him.

Harry crawled toward the gun and pried it free from Cliff's dead fingers. With no hesitation, Harry whirled the barrel of the weapon into the direction of the wood ape and prepared himself to do what was necessary to protect his daughter. Much to his dismay, he found that the creature had already snatched up Alice and was lumbering back toward him. She was cradled against the wood ape's chest, and Harry was unable to fire the weapon where he'd initially wanted. He lowered the weapon, deciding he'd have to settle on injuring one of the creature's legs instead when suddenly, the last thing he expected to happen, happened.

The wood ape towered over him but dropped to one knee when it was a few feet away from Harry. Instead of harming Alice, the beast carefully placed Alice on the ground in front of it. The wood ape then gently pushed the girl toward Harry. He instinctively grabbed her and jerked her toward him, all the while moving backward to put more distance between himself and the beast. The wood ape only snorted in response and looked on as

Harry moved backward up the slope. Just as he was about to lose sight of the creature, the wood ape grabbed the corpse of Cliff Lowe and dragged it away to a darkened corner of the chamber. The last thing Harry heard as he stepped into the sunlight was the tearing of flesh echoing from within the darkness of the hut.

EPILOGUE

Three Months Later...

Harry pushed back from his desk and rubbed at his eyes. He was exhausted and staring at the bright computer screen did nothing to help the matter. He rubbed at his eyes and yawned, deciding that if there was any chance of getting his work done, he'd have to get up and move around to get his blood flowing. He was thankful for the Baker County School Districts willingness to allow him more flexibility with his work schedule, so he could receive his treatments and work from home on the days where he felt extraordinarily weak. Today was one of those days.

Dwight had recovered completely from his injuries and was more than eager to return to his life on the road. Harry supposed it would be a long time before he returned to Baker County Mississippi, and he seriously doubted if his brother in law would ever venture into a forest again. Once Harry had come clean with Lacey about his cancer, the strain their marriage had been under began to improve. He felt tremendous guilt for keeping her in the dark, especially when he realized how strongly she believed he was having an affair. *That*, he later explained, was the furthest thing from his mind.

Alice, much like her brother, had sustained a concussion at the hands of the wood ape, but otherwise was unharmed—at least physically. Unfortunately, there were numerous nights where Harry and Lacey were awoken to the screams of their daughter as the wood ape continued to haunt her in her dreams. She'd begun seeing a child psychiatrist and Harry had begun to see slow progress. He sincerely hoped she wouldn't be scarred for life.

It was a beautiful sunny day and he decided he'd take a walk outside for some fresh air. Harry stepped out onto the front porch and was surprised to find that Sheriff Travis Horne had just pulled up, the dust that had been trailing his car rolling in as the vehicle came to a halt.

"How are you doing, Harry?" the sheriff asked, slamming the car door behind him.

Harry forced a smile and sat down on the porch swing, motioning for Horne to join him. Truthfully, he was growing tired of the sheriff's weekly visits, but he allowed the man to continue them as it was obvious he felt extreme guilt for everything that occurred to the Schrader family since their arrival in Baker County.

"I told you that you don't have to keep stopping by," Harry said as Horne climbed the porch steps.

The sheriff removed his hat and sighed before finally taking a seat on a nearby rocking chair. "I know what you said," he replied, staring at the star on the front of his hat. "And I told you to let me do what I need to do to reconcile with everything that's happened."

Harry eyed the man a moment before finally allowing his gaze to drift across the meadow and finally to the dense forest beyond it. He said nothing.

"I'm not going to sit on the sidelines and pretend that this craziness isn't happening any longer," Horne continued. "I've gotten the Mississippi Department of Fish and Game involved and they are all over this part of the county. Sooner or later, we'll catch it, and then we'll kill it."

Harry chuckled and shook his head. Sheriff Horne turned to look at him. "You're not going to catch it," Harry said, matter-of-factly. "If Clifford Lowe, a man that had collected decades of information on the thing couldn't stop it, then I'm sorry, but I don't have a lot of confidence in you or the Mississippi Department of Fish and Game doing it either."

Sheriff Horne scowled and looked across the meadow to where Harry had been staring. They both thought of the rogue wood ape and wondered if it was staring back at them from somewhere beyond the shadows.

"You're sure you're comfortable still living here?" Horne asked.

Harry shook his head. "Of course not," he answered. "However, I'm not nearly as hard to convince as Lacey. It's taken a lot of assurances from me to convince her to stay. Some days I wonder if she's gonna leave me because of it truthfully."

The sheriff glanced over at him, taken aback. "That bad, huh?"

Harry's eyes widened, and he inhaled deeply through his nose. "Well, maybe not quite *that* bad," he said. "But, she was attacked by that thing and I was attacked by that thing. Alice and Dwight were both kidnapped by that thing. It made it very clear right after we arrived here that it wanted us. Even though I'd tried my best to convince her that it's going to leave us alone now, she won't allow herself to get comfortable with the situation. Honestly, I can't blame her."

Sheriff Horne huffed and shook his head. "Then why are you so hell-bent on staying?" he asked, puzzled.

Harry looked at him. "Well, first and foremost, this place isn't going to be easy to sell. Especially since all the locals are aware of what's gone on over here. It was on the market a long time before we were dumb enough to buy it. I'm under no illusion that we'd be able to sell it any faster."

"That can't be the only reason," the sheriff replied. "If I'd been in your shoes, I'd have long since had a FOR SALE sign in the front yard."

Harry shrugged. "Well, it's like I've been telling you. The wood ape isn't going to be bothering us anymore."

The sheriff chuckled and shook his head in disbelief. "Yeah, I know you keep saying that, but you can't give me a good reason why that would be the case."

"Because it had its chance with me and decided it didn't want me. I'm tainted."

Sheriff Horne's eyes narrowed. "What are you talking about? The cancer?"

Harry nodded. "Cliff told me one time that those things are finicky eaters. It sniffed me up and down really good when it was trying to decide if it wanted to eat me. I think it could smell the cancer and ultimately decided I wasn't worth eating."

Sheriff Horne smiled. "Are you saying that the cancer is what ended up saving you?"

Harry nodded again. "I think a lot of things happen for reasons we don't fully understand until later. I think that I ended up with cancer because one day I was going to come face to face with that monster. In the end, the cancer saved me."

"Okay," Horne replied, unconvinced. "Then why didn't it eat Alice?"

Harry shrugged and crossed his arms. He again looked across the meadow toward the forest. "I'm not really sure about that," he answered. "I've thought about it and all I can really come up with is that perhaps it thought she was infected too."

"And you think this is the reason that it won't be bothering you anymore?"

"Pretty much," Harry replied. "Now I've just got to beat the cancer."

"How is that going?"

Harry returned his attention to the sheriff and ran a hand over his bald head. "Well, I'm taking the treatments, so time will tell," he answered. "I figure I didn't escape certain death at the hands of the wood ape for no reason at all. I think I'll beat the cancer and get on with my life, right here in Baker County."

Sheriff Horne smiled and nodded. "Well, we're glad to have you here."

Harry chuckled. "Seems like I've heard that before."

"Well, this time I mean it," Horne said, rising from his seat. "Whether you believe it not, I'm going to put an end to this. We're going to catch that Squatch, dead or alive."

Harry nodded, but it was obvious he didn't believe him. "Good luck, Sheriff."

Sheriff Horne tipped his hat, strolled back down the steps, and got into his squad car. As he drove toward Isley Road, he was forced to momentarily stop. A massive heavy gate rolled slowly out of the way to allow him to leave the Schrader property. The newly installed fencing was twelve feet high, made of iron, and completely surrounded the old antebellum house the Schrader's now called home. Clearly, Harry wasn't as comfortable that the rogue wood ape would not return as he'd wanted the sheriff to believe.

The End

SEVERED**PRESS**

f facebook.com/severedpress
y twitter.com/severedpress

HECK OUT OTHER GREAT
ORROR NOVELS

BLACK FRIDAY
by Michael Hodges

Jared the kleptomaniac, Chike the unemployed IT guy, Patricia the shopaholic, and Jeff the meth dealer are trapped inside a Chicago supermall on Black Friday. Bridgefield Mall empties during a fire alarm, and most of the shoppers drive off into a strange mist surrounding the mall parking lot. They never return. Chike and his group try calling friends and family, but their smart phones won't work, not even Twitter. As the mist creeps closer, the mall lights flicker and surge. Bulbs shatter and spray glass into the air. Unsettling noises are heard from within the mist, as the meth dealer becomes unhinged and hunts the group within the mall. Cornered by the mist, and hunted from within, Chike and the survivors must fight for their lives while solving the mystery of what happened to Bridgefield Mall. Sometimes, a good sale just isn't worth it.

GRIMWEAVE
by Tim Curran

In the deepest, darkest jungles of Indochina, an ancient evil is waiting in a forgotten, primeval valley. It is patient, monstrous, and bloodthirsty. Perfectly adapted to its hot, steaming environment, it strikes silent and stealthy, it chosen prey: human. Now Michael Spiers, a Marine sniper, the only survivor of a previous encounter with the beast, is going after it again. Against his better judgement, he is made part of a Marine Force Recon team that will hunt it down and destroy it.

The hunters are about to become the hunted.

 SEVERED**PRESS**

f facebook.com/severedpr

twitter.com/severedpress

CHECK OUT OTHER GREAT
HORROR NOVELS

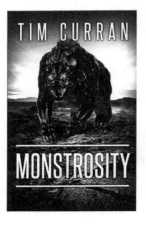

MONSTROSITY
by Tim Curran

The Food. It seeped from the ground, a living, gushing teratogenic nightmare. It contaminated anything that ate it causing nature to run wild with horrible mutations, creating massive monstrosities that roam the land destroying towns and cities, feeding on livestock and human beings and one another. Now Frank Bowman, an ordinary farmer with no military skills, must get his children to safety. And that will mean a trip through the contaminated zone of monsters madmen, and The Food itself. Only a fool would attempt it Or a man with a mission.

THE SQUIRMING
by Jack Hamlyn

You are their hosts

You are their food.

The parasites came out of nowhere, squirming horrors that enslaved the human race.They turned the population into mindless pack animals, psychotic cannibalistic hordes whose only purpose was to feed them.

Now with the human race teetering at the edge of extinction, extermination teams are fighting back, killing off the parasites and their voracious hosts. Taking them out one by one in violent, bloody encounters.

The future of mankind is at stake.

And time is running out.

SEVERED**PRESS**

f facebook.com/severedpress
**twitter.com/severedpress

HECK OUT OTHER GREAT
ORROR NOVELS

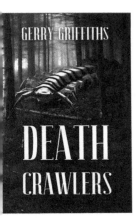

DEATH CRAWLERS
by Gerry Griffiths

Worldwide, there are thought to be 8,000 species of centipede, of which, only 3,000 have been scientifically recorded. The venom of Scolopendra gigantea—the largest of the arthropod genus found in the Amazon rainforest—is so potent that it is fatal to small animals and toxic to humans. But when a cargo plane departs the Amazon region and crashes inside a national park in the United States, much larger and deadlier creatures escape the wreckage to roam wild, reproducing at an astounding rate. Entomologist, Frank Travis solicits small town sheriff Wanda Rafferty's help and together they investigate the crash site. But as a rash of gruesome deaths befalls the townsfolk of Prospect, Frank and Wanda will soon discover how vicious and cunning these new breed of predators can be. Meanwhile, Jake and Nora Carver, and another backpacking couple, are venturing up into the mountainous terrain of the park. If only they knew their fun-filled weekend is about to become a living nightmare.

THE PULLER
by Michael Hodges

Matt Kearns has two choices: fight or hide. The creature in the orchard took the rest. Three days ago, he arrived at his favorite place in the world, a remote shack in Michigan's Upper Peninsula. The plan was to mourn his father's death and figure out his life. Now he's fighting for it. An invisible creature has him trapped. Every time Matt tries to flee, he's dragged backwards by an unseen force. Alone and with no hope of rescue, Matt must escape the Puller's reach. But how do you free yourself from something you cannot see?

CPSIA information can be obtained
at www.ICGtesting.com
Printed in the USA
LVHW081231140922
728279LV00002B/237

9 781925 840l